HARD IMPACT

Matt Rogers

CHAPTER 1

0700 hours.

One hundred miles from Iquitos, Peru.

Waiting was the worst part.

Jason King tucked his knees further into his chest. He rocked back and forth, slowly and steadily. His heart hammered. In times like these, the fear began to surface. It didn't matter how many operations he had been through. It didn't matter how many times he had narrowly escaped death.

The fear never left.

He sat on the padded floor of a tiny single-engine plane. A Cessna 182. The only other occupant was the pilot, Diego, a wiry Peruvian man with a pencil moustache and long dreadlocked hair. He chewed absent-mindedly on a toothpick as he flew. The small aircraft rocked and shook as the wind outside battered against its panels, but it didn't seem to bother him in the slightest. King was also unperturbed. If the plane went down, he would not be around to see it.

The straps on his shoulders dug tight, connected to the parachute container on his back. A constant reminder that there was nothing but a large canopy separating him from survival and certain death. Especially in these conditions.

Landing would be a bitch.

'Thirty seconds,' Diego said in heavily accented English.

'You sure about the landing zone?' he said.

'You will be fine, brother. I don't know about rest of mission. But if you jump when I say, you live. Simple?'

'Simple,' King repeated in an attempt to reassure himself.

The Cessna flew fourteen-thousand feet above the Amazon Rainforest. King leaned over and glanced out the dirty side window. Nothing but a sea of green in all directions. Over five million square miles of dense jungle, much of it unexplored.

Ten seconds from now, he would freefall into uncharted territory.

'Ready?' Diego said, one hand tapping a glass display next to the controls. 'Almost there.'

'Ready,' King said.

An uncontrollable burst of adrenalin flooded through his veins. He had given up on trying to manage the feeling long ago. Jumping out of a plane was something that you couldn't get used to. Each time it came with the vertigo and the rushing wind and the awe and the terror.

King checked his gear a final time. Parachute on his back, packed meticulously inside its container. Duffel bag locked against his chest, fastened securely. Inside the bag was a FN SCAR-17 assault rifle, a Heckler and Koch MP5SD sub-machine gun with attached suppressor, a Glock 19 compact pistol, countless rounds of ammunition, several all-weather insect-repellent khakis, a handful of ration packs, some water purifying tablets and a small machete.

That was it, apart from the second Glock 19 strapped to a holster at his waist.

It was unclear how long this operation would take, but if he needed more supplies than that, he knew his position would be in jeopardy. He hit targets fast, and he hit them hard. Spending too long planning led to delays. Delays killed momentum.

This line of thinking explained the arsenal he had chosen for the jungle. Soldiers of his calibre — of which there were few — often spent hours selecting tailor-made, customised weapons. These were usually prototypes reserved for the upper echelons of the special forces.

Not King.

He saw nothing but potential problems in guns like that. The majority of them were largely untested. He favoured the sturdiest, most reliable weaponry available. The guns that would never in a million years jam on the battlefield, in the heat of combat.

'Door!' Diego screamed.

King had lost count of the number of times he'd heard that same command. For as long as he could remember, he'd operated alone. That meant clandestine missions. It meant sneaking around behind enemy lines without any of his foe having the slightest notion that he was there. It meant using unconventional methods to enter hostile situations.

Usually he came from the sky.

He reached for the handle and threw the door up and outward. In came the screaming wind, howling around the tiny cabin, shaking the plane to its core. It deafened him. But with it came an icy calmness. It was time to act.

No more waiting around.

No more nerves.

He slapped the pilot on the shoulder, gesturing good-bye. Diego raised a hand, thumb pointing towards the roof of the plane. They had known each other for less than an hour. Something about the tension of dawning combat created a bond.

Then King stepped out onto the tiny foothold. He looked down once, and it tightened his gut. The treetops were dots. Rivers snaked across the terrain like string. It was all so far away. Wind battered him relentlessly, threatening to throw him off the ledge he was perched on. It didn't bother him. He would leap off on his own accord soon enough.

Head up. Back arched.

Go.

He stepped off into nothingness.

CHAPTER 2

C.F. Secada International Airport.
  Iquitos, Peru.
  Twelve hours earlier…

The sun had just dipped below the horizon as the passenger plane touched down on the runway. It carried more than a hundred passengers, almost entirely tourists. One of the flight attendants read a pleasant welcome announcement over the speakers as it pulled up to the terminal next to the few other arrivals.

Jason King was displeased. The flight had been rough and the food had been terrible. He had not slept for more than sixteen hours. A long day of travel lay behind him. He wasn't sure what lay ahead.

The seatbelt lights overhead flicked off simultaneously. King rose from the economy-class seat he had spent the last ten hours in and grabbed his sole piece of luggage. A single khaki backpack. In it were the only possessions he ever carried with him while he travelled between operations.

That's how he spent his life. At the service of whichever high-ranking official needed him. Sent across the globe, dropped into the middle of warzones. A combat operative for one of the most secretive and exclusive government departments on the planet.

Black Force.

He was under no illusion as to how important he was. No-one else could do what he did. No-one else survived what he had, sometimes a hair's breadth from death. Somehow, he always found a way to get the job done.

'Thanks for flying with us,' the flight attendant said as he strode past into the detachable corridor.

It pulled him out of his thoughts. 'Thank you.'

He was the first one off the plane. He always was. Everyone else moved so ... slowly. Their actions seemed laborious. Like they had all the time in the world. Perhaps they did. King certainly did not.

As he stepped out into the terminal, he scanned his surroundings. It was peak hour at the airport. Approaching seven in the evening. Tourists bustled to and fro, munching on fast food and sorting through boarding documents.

A man loitered by the walkway he had come through. He wore plain blue jeans, slightly faded, and a brown leather jacket over a white V-neck shirt. He was white, with plain features: a receding hairline, round glasses and a shadow of a beard. Nothing about him stood out. But King knew that was the intention. He held a small placard that read: *'GERARD STEVENS.'*

King stopped in front of him. 'That's me.'

'Gerard?' the man said, his expression quizzical.

'The one and only.'

'Excellent, we have a car waiting for you. My name is Clint. Would you like me to accompany you to collect your luggage?'

'I've already got it.'

'Where is it?'

King motioned to the pack slung over one shoulder. 'Here.'

Clint nodded. 'Of course. Right this way.'

They dodged hordes of civilians passing through the terminal. All of them either heading toward airport security or the departure gates. As they approached the lines for the metal detectors, Clint pushed past the crowd. He made eye contact with the officer manning the computer. Pointed a single finger at King. The officer gave a curt nod and ushered them straight through, without any question.

'You're well-known,' King said as they headed for the exit.

'Not really. They don't have much idea what's going on.'

'They sure are co-operative.'

'Of course. A phone call from the President changes a lot of things.'

As they stepped foot outside, the first thing King noticed was the heat. Beads of sweat appeared on his forehead. He wiped them away with the sleeve of his T-shirt. The humidity threatened to turn his skin damp within a minute.

'Please tell me your ride's close,' King said.

'Very. Special privileges.'

He breathed a sigh of relief. They crossed the asphalt in front of the terminal and entered a small car park.

'Here we are,' Clint said, unlocking a battered sedan with an electronic key. The vehicle looked as if it would fall apart at any moment.

'Fuck me,' King said. 'The budget must have been enormous for this operation.'

'We spared no expense for you,' Clint said, a little curtly. 'Doesn't matter what the rest of us have. We're not the ones risking our lives.'

'You sure aren't.'

King threw his bag into the back as he climbed in. Left out in the sun for a period of time, the interior of the sedan was an inferno. The air felt heavy. It was impossible to stop the perspiration seeping out of his pores.

'Where are we headed?' he asked as Clint fired up the engine.

'An airfield on the other side of the city. Much more secluded. We've organised a private plane to fly you to the drop-off point. I'm one half of your assistance detail. The other guy will meet us there.'

'Are you briefing me? Because right now I know as much as those airport guards.'

'That's Brad's job. He's waiting for us with the mission file. It's got everything you need to know.'

'Do you have my gear?'

Clint nodded. 'Everything's ready to go.'

'Perfect.'

King settled back and observed the urban life in Peru. It was far from pretty. Clint drove through dirty streets strewn with rubbish. The sidewalks were damp. The air bore down heavier in the heart of the city. Thick and musty. Hot and wet. By now the sun had disappeared completely. He sweltered in the evening heat.

Faint streetlights flickered on and off, partially illuminating the roads. The pedestrians they passed ranged from young children to elderly beggars. Most seemed happy. They were used to the conditions.

'So you're Jason King,' Clint said after a long period of silence.

'I am.'

'It's weird to finally meet you in the flesh.'

'How so?'

'Well, you know … everyone talks about you. But you're a myth. No-one ever sees you.'

'That's because I work alone.'

'Who for, exactly? Everyone in Delta knows you because you used to be one of us. Then they whisked you off for some secret project. Now no-one has a fucking clue what you do.'

'I'm not with a branch of the military. I guess you could say I'm an independent contractor.'

'To who?'

'The very top. I can't go into too much detail.'

'I understand.'

Another quiet moment. Very faintly, far in the distance, King thought he heard a gunshot. He twitched at the sound.

'Don't worry,' Clint said. 'That's just Iquitos.'

King didn't respond. It was now dark outside. 'What time are wheels up?'

'You fly out at 0500.'

'Into the jungle?'

'Do you really know nothing about your operation?'

'Like I said, I haven't been briefed.'

'I don't know how the fuck you do it.'

King looked at him. 'Do what?'

'You're a madman. You fly from country to country doing whatever people tell you. You constantly put your life on the line. You don't stop. I mean, the stories I've heard...'

'I'm not a regular guy,' King said. 'Far from it. I can't stay in one place for too long. I get restless. I can't sleep. I feel useless. I need to be moving.'

Clint shook his head. 'Doesn't all this scare the shit out of you?'

'Of course it does. That's the point.'

'What?'

'Doing what frightens me keeps me going. I never know what I'm walking into. Every time they send me somewhere, I go in expecting to die.'

'You're insane. I'm an analyst, for Christ's sake, and all this still scares me.'

'So it should. It's a dangerous game.'

'Well, you seem to be comfortable in it.'

'Far from it. But I'm one of the rare people who gets a kick out of being uncomfortable.'

'A lot of people embrace being uncomfortable. They take up extreme sports, or push themselves out of their comfort zone. They don't go charging into a warzone.'

'Maybe that's how I stay sane. I feel like I'm wasting away if I don't live on the edge.'

Clint scoffed. 'Unbelievable. Well, whatever gets you through the day.'

He hit the gas and the sedan lurched forward, roaring to the airfield.

CHAPTER 3

Slowly, the urban buildings on either side grew further and further apart. Another ten minutes of travel and they were out of the centre of Iquitos. It was quieter out this way. No constant drone of traffic. Just crickets and the buzz of the streetlights, occasionally interspersed with distant yelling.

'Where are you headed after you send me off?' King said.

'Back to HQ.'

'Where's that?'

'Texas.'

'You spend a lot of time there?'

'Most of it. This globe-trotting thing is new to me.'

'It makes you uneasy. I can tell.'

'Like I said, I'm just an analyst. I'm not used to field work.'

'After this, you're done,' King said. 'You'll watch my plane fly out and then you'll head back to the airport and get on a plane home. Safe and sound.'

'I can't even imagine how you feel.'

'Reserved. I'm used to this.'

'I hope they pay well.'

'They do. But that's not the point.'

Clint stopped outside a wire fence that seemed to run forever. Overgrown weeds snaked through the gaps down low. There was a gate in front of them, manned by a Peruvian guard in a dishevelled uniform. King noticed the pistol in a holster at his belt. Clint stuck an arm out the open driver's window and held his palm out, fingers spread. A wave. The guard nodded, much like the airport security officer had, and moved to open the gate for them. Their headlights illuminated the space directly ahead, but the rest was darkness. King saw a field of dead grass stretching out in all directions.

The guard opened the gate and waved them through. He said nothing as the sedan crawled slowly past.

Tension ran thick in the air. King recognised it. The guard's airfield had been rented out by persons unknown, for reasons unknown. The man would not have been told what was happening. He had been kept in the dark, forced to stand around waiting to open the gate for mysterious men in the shadows. King often imagined these scenarios from the perspective of outsiders.

The sedan tackled the overgrown grass reasonably well. The sky had turned black, and the only light in these parts came from the headlights. Twin beams lit up the path ahead like beacons. They revealed nothing but flat ground as far as King could see.

'You said this was an airfield,' he said.

'It is. I didn't say it was well-kept.'

Eventually they hit a runway, the tarmac cracked and damaged. King wondered how planes took off from its surface.

He would find out in the morning.

The sudden silence was eerie. They'd made the trip to the airfield through the bustling heart of Iquitos, surrounded by the sounds of the city. Now there was nothing. The only noise came from the sedan's grumbling engine.

Then he saw a faint source of light in the distance. A yellow glow. Windows, far away.

'Is that us?' he said.

Clint nodded. 'It's where we've set up camp. The airplane hangar. Don't get excited, it's nothing interesting.'

King realised that as they pulled up to the entrance. "Hangar" was a very loose definition of the building that lay ahead. It was a warehouse made of corrugated iron. Its walls were in the process of rusting away. The entire structure looked like it could collapse from a slight gust of wind. The roller doors were up, revealing the inside of the building, illuminated softly by flickering overhead lights. A single space, high ceilings, cracked concrete floor. It seemed like everything was broken around these parts. A dirty single-engine plane sat in the centre, surrounded by vast open space.

A Cessna, King noted.

Next to that a cluster of trestle tables had been erected, their surfaces strewn with documents and laptop computers. A man sat in a folding chair at the tables. The hangar's only occupant.

As King and Clint pulled inside, he rose off his seat and came over. He seemed a similar age to Clint, with a full head of thick hair and a tanned, weather-beaten face. He wore a loose long-sleeved shirt. The sleeves were rolled up to his elbows, revealing muscular forearms. He had the soldier look in his eyes. It was a difficult emotion to describe, but King never failed to recognise it. A mixture of determination and constant alertness. The look of a man who never truly switched off.

'Brad,' Clint said as he climbed out of the car. 'This is Jason King.'

They shook hands. Brad had a firm grip.

'How are you?' King said.

'Who gives a fuck?' Brad said. 'You don't care how I am. I'm here to brief you. Then you're off. That's it.'

'Good,' King said. 'We think alike. I really don't give a fuck how you are.'

Brad nodded. Mutual respect. 'Perfect. Let's get to work.'

They moved to the tables. As they walked, Clint took a detour to the side of the hangar and grabbed a remote hanging from the wall. He pressed a single button and the roller doors began descending, accompanied by an almighty screeching noise.

'What do you know about what you're heading into?' Brad said.

'Absolutely nothing,' King said.

Brad raised an eyebrow. 'You've got nerves of steel.'

'Maybe I don't. Maybe when I find out what I'm facing I'll hightail it out of here and catch a flight back home.'

'I doubt it. Rumours are you never turn down anything.'

King said nothing. Simply nodded. Sometimes, rumours proved correct.

'Okay,' Brad said, staring down at the files in front of him. 'First things first. The Fantasmas De La Selva.'

King knew rudimentary Spanish. He translated in his head. 'Jungle Phantoms?'

'That's what they call themselves. Sounds spooky. Really they're just a gang of drug runners operating out of a facility somewhere in the Amazon.'

'You don't know where?'

'We know roughly where. That's the crux of this whole operation. These slimy fuckers are responsible for eighty percent of the cocaine in Iquitos. And, quite frankly, they're very good at what they do. They have a horde of men in the city distributing. They have runners transporting the drugs from the rainforest to the city. They have who knows how many men in the jungle itself, protecting their warehouse. And the entire thing is so well-oiled that they've been doing this for the last three years without detection.'

'What do we have to do with this?' King said. 'Sounds like a problem for the police.'

It was a harsh statement, but a necessary one. There were thousands of drug gangs across the globe, each wreaking havoc in their own respective regions. King was a specialist, and he could not tackle them all. Some situations were a matter for the local authorities.

'It was their problem,' Brad said. 'They've been doing everything they can to put a stop to the operation. Crime rates have been rising. There's more and more addicts on the streets. It's turning into a crisis. The police were sinking all their resources into locating their HQ in the rainforest, and they were close.'

'Were?'

'The Phantoms realised the cops were catching up. They got desperate. There's been a pattern of killings in the last week. Thirty-seven in total, all gunned down in the street. We think they're people who had information on the Phantoms in one way or the other. Basically, anyone suspected of leaking anything is getting executed. Doesn't matter if they did it. Doesn't matter what they knew. They're covering their tracks ruthlessly.

'Then, the cops thought they had something. They'd compiled enough data and surveillance to conclude the rough whereabouts of the facility. They didn't know exactly what they were up against, so they brought the files to the US embassy in Lima. A request for help. This was yesterday.'

'Fuck,' King said. He knew where Brad was heading. 'Were they followed?'

Brad nodded. 'A truck full of armed men opened fire on the embassy as soon as the officers walked through the front door. Then they stormed the place. All the cops from Iquitos are dead. Four of ours are dead. The whole place is trashed. And they took three embassy workers hostage. All ours.'

No-one spoke. The walls of the hangar creaked, battered by the night wind outside. King couldn't shake a sinking feeling in his gut that this was unresolvable without massive violence.

CHAPTER 4

King took a moment to mull over the information he had just received. It was a volatile situation. Any action involving embassies crossed all kinds of lines. The reaction would be catastrophic.

He calmly organised his thoughts, until the most pressing question came to mind.

'Who knows?' he said.

'Not the media,' Brad said. 'We've managed to keep this under wraps for now. It'll come out eventually, of course.'

'That's impossible,' King said. 'Armed men shoot up an embassy and no-one knows about it?'

'They know something's happened. But we cordoned off the scene before any of them got there. It's a high-walled compound. They can't see in. They're running around the exterior, harassing us for details. That's it so far.'

'Do you know where they took the hostages?'

'We do. These guys are ruthless, but they're idiots. They've uploaded a video on a private site they knew we would find. They think they're a step ahead. Want to watch?'

King nodded.

Brad spun one of the laptops around to face him and tapped the space bar, starting a video. The camera quality was grainy and pixelated, but it wasn't hard to make out the three Americans tied to chairs, hessian sacks over their heads, all perched on the floor of a grimy, dark warehouse. A long rectangular window in the background showed dense foliage. The vegetation outside was a stark green.

'They took them into the jungle?' King said.

'They did. Must have taken them all last night to make the journey. Luckily, we still have the documents the cops brought to our embassy. We know roughly where their facility is.'

A man behind the camera began to talk in stunted English. His voice was deep and heavily accented.

'We have three American,' the voice said. 'The authorities will leave us alone. If any of us are arrested, we kill American. If any interference *at all*, we kill American. Embassy was sending message. You leave us *alone*, or next time is worse.'

The image froze, signifying the end of the video.

King turned to look at Brad. 'Surely they know that will only create a shitstorm.'

'Like I said, they're idiots. They think we don't know their location. But we do. And that's where you come in.'

'Hang on,' King said. 'Have you done any surveillance?'

'We can't. Their whole compound's covered by the rainforest canopy. We did some drone scouting and found nothing. But they're definitely near a set of co-ordinates we have. That much we know.'

'This is one of the worst-researched plans I've ever come across.'

'Well we need you, King, or they'll kill the hostages on video and broadcast it to the world just as the media's releasing information on what happened at the embassy. We're trying to prevent a massive overreaction, because if this goes public, you can be damn sure someone is going to.'

'Send in a team.'

'We can't. They'll pick up our scent. And you've seen that they're not afraid to kill on the slightest whim.'

'So the main priority is rescuing the hostages?'

'That's paramount. Retrieve all three of them alive. Anything else is a secondary objective. If you kill hostiles, fine. No-one's going to prosecute you for that. No-one will even know you were there if this all goes according to plan.'

'I take it this is off the books.'

'Completely.'

'Is there backup?'

'You're looking at it. Anything goes wrong, the two of us will extract you.'

'That's a confidence booster if I've ever heard one.'

'Get fucked.'

'Who are the hostages?'

Brad used the trackpad on the laptop to open a folder of photos. He tapped three times, bringing up three passport photos on the screen, side by side. Two men and a woman.

The man on the left was bald, with a permanent scowl. He looked like he had previously served. Brad pointed at him: 'Roman Woodford. Ex-military. He was security for the embassy. They killed all the other guards.'

'He could help if I get him out,' King noted.

The woman in the middle looked secretarial. She had shoulder-length blond hair, tied back. She looked to be in her late forties. 'Jodi Burns,' Brad said. 'She co-ordinated diplomatic relations. She's tough, according to her co-workers. Resilient.'

'What about this kid?' King said, motioning to the male on the right. *Kid *was the correct choice of word. He had a young, boyish face and slicked back auburn hair. 'He looks like he should still be in school.'

'He *is* in school,' Brad said. 'Studying international relations at the University of Tennessee. His name's Ben Norton. He was two months into an internship at the embassy when this happened. He's the real worry. If the media finds out they have him hostage, this thing will explode.'

King paused. Pointed at the photo of Ben Norton. 'It will be disastrous if anything happens to him. Emotions will be high. Reactions will be reckless.'

'I know.'

'Okay…' King said, taking a deep breath. 'I need to go in, get these three out, kill as many of the Phantoms as I can and get extracted. How do I do that?'

'A pilot will meet us at this hangar at 0500,' Brad said. 'He'll fly you to the exact co-ordinates the embassy gave us and you'll skydive in, with gear.'

'In this?' King said, slapping the hull of the Cessna.

'Yes. Then you locate the facility, do your thing and call us when you need extraction. There's a Delta chopper on its way to Iquitos. It'll be ready by the time you're done tomorrow. We had limited resources as to how to get you in there.'

'Hang on,' King said. 'Limited resources. Are you telling me the pilot's not one of us?'

'He's not military. He's a private contractor, working out of this airfield. It was the best we could do given the circumstances.'

'Why isn't he running his little business out of the airport?'

'He lost his license three months ago, for flying intoxicated. The customers he sells tourist packages to don't know that though.'

'Jesus.'

'It's how we bribed him into helping us.'

King said nothing.

'Are you in, King?' Brad said.

The hangar lapsed into silence. Clearly, they expected him to speak. He stayed quiet. Resting one hand on the Cessna. Thinking hard. The reason for his massive success on the battlefield and ability to avoid death like it was a mere inconvenience was due to years upon years of calculated and efficient assessment. He had to know exactly what to do and when to do it. If this operation went ahead, it would only be after his approval. He had the facts in his head. Now it was time to weigh them.

The two men watched him intently. They knew not to interrupt. They recognised the look. The absolute concentration.

Finally, he spoke.

'Okay.'

Brad nodded. 'Get some rest, King. It's going to be a tough day tomorrow.'

'I'm aware of that. Where do I sleep?'

They showed him through to a small room built into the rear wall of the hangar. It contained nothing but a bare mattress, devoid of sheets or bedding, and a small sink for washing up. King remained unperturbed. He had slept in infinitely worse conditions before. A mattress would do fine, no matter how thin or unkempt.

'We'll wake you at 0400,' Brad said.

'I'll be awake,' King said.

He heard them leave and shut the door behind them. After all this time, he was alone. He would use these hours to recharge his batteries and calm himself for the operation ahead. Despite what many thought, he was an introvert. He had no trouble conversing with people, but when left to his own devices he could take some time to wind down and zone in. Being alone energised him. It was why he had operated by himself for all these years. He was not suited for a team environment. His success came from making decisions himself, instantaneously, without having to debate their merits with others. In combat his judgments were always precise, and not having to relay that to fellow soldiers was a key component of his ability to survive.

He lay down on the mattress and shut his eyes. Within seconds he was asleep.

CHAPTER 5

Clint and Brad re-entered the room at exactly 0400. As promised.

King was already awake. As promised.

He sat on the bed, dressed in a plain white T-shirt and jeans. He hadn't paid any attention to his clothing. He knew it would be replaced by tactical gear imminently.

'Lovely morning, isn't it?' he said as the door swung inwards.

'Did you set an alarm?' Brad said, taking a look around the room.

'I didn't bring a phone,' King said. 'I never bring anything personal on these operations. Helps detach myself from regular life.'

'How did you wake up so early naturally?'

'I never sleep long.'

Too many bad dreams. Too many violent memories.

Brad seemed to sense that he wasn't getting much else out of King. 'Alright. Follow us. Let's get you ready.'

King trailed behind the pair as they headed out of the makeshift bedroom. It was still dark in Iquitos. The halogen lights overhead seemed to flicker even worse than the previous night. As they walked, King noted that Clint had not said a word to him since they had entered the airfield six hours ago. He believed what the man had said on the drive there. Clandestine operations in Peru were most definitely stretching the limits of his comfort zone.

'We were told to supply you with the same gear you use on every assignment,' Brad said, waving his hands toward a thick grey duffel bag sitting atop the closest trestle table. 'Plus jungle survival tools, of course.'

'I hope you packed the minimum.'

'We did. As instructed.'

'Are you nervous?' Clint said quietly.

'Very,' King said.

'You're not showing it.'

'I can't afford to. Have to keep up appearances. Everyone will tell you the tough-guy act is just that, an act. Even Brad here.'

The soldier shrugged. 'Everyone gets scared.'

'Damn right they do. I'm just as scared as you would be, Clint.'

'I doubt that,' Clint said.

'It's a controlled fear. Do this job enough and everyone would grow numb.'

'I wouldn't.'

'You'll never know until you try it.'

King spent the next half hour meticulously analysing the contents of the duffel bag. He performed the same actions every time, without fail. Routine meant no mistakes. It meant he would not head straight into territory and find his gun jammed, or his ammunition low, or any of the other thousand possibilities that could occur in the heat of combat. He disassembled all four of his weapons. Checked each individual part for flaws. He made sure to take extreme patience and care with the tasks. There was a time for brashness and recklessness. It wasn't before the mission began.

Brad strode over as the time approached 0500.

'They work,' he said, motioning to the guns King was in the process of reassembling. 'Trust me.'

'I do trust you. Doesn't mean I shouldn't check for myself.'

Brad shrugged. 'Doesn't affect me.'

'How will I keep in contact during the mission?'

Brad gestured to a trio of thick satellite phones on the edge of the table ahead. 'Take one of those. They work anywhere on the planet. If you truly need backup, call. But only if shit hits the fan.'

'Where's our pilot?'

'He should be here right about —' Brad glanced down at his chunky digital wrist watch '—now.'

Not a sound. There was no sign of any new arrivals for the following ten minutes. King spent the time packing his gear back into the duffel bag. Not rushing, making sure everything fit just right. Clint paced restlessly back and forth across the path of the roller doors, which he had raised when the clock hit five in the morning. A small arc of runway was visible, faintly illuminated by the glow of the hangar's lights. On the horizon, the faint shimmer of light began to appear.

Another ten minutes passed.

Still nothing.

'I told him to be here at five on the dot,' Brad said, shaking his head. His tone had become exasperated.

'He's a civilian,' King said. 'He's probably not as strict about these things as we are. Doesn't realise the urgency. You didn't tell him anything about what we're doing, did you?'

'Of course not.'

'Then give him time. There's no use panicking over things we can't control.'

But even King began to grow wary when 0530 came and went. By now, Clint was a nervous wreck.

'We're completely fucked if he doesn't show,' Clint said, his voice cracking with each syllable. He ran two hands through his thinning hair. 'I'm not exaggerating. Command will tear us apart. This was on us to organise, Brad. We told them we could handle it.'

'Shut the fuck up,' Brad said. His voice cut through the hangar like a knife. 'He'll be here.'

King waited patiently. Silently. His mind was elsewhere.

In the distance, the drone of an engine.

'Oh, thank God,' Clint said.

Sure enough, it was the pilot. He drove a beat-up pickup truck, paint flaking off its sides. The vehicle looked worse off than Clint's sedan as it bounced over the runway toward the hangar. Even from this distance, King could tell the suspension was terrible.

The sun had just started to rise, turning the sky yellow. He walked with Brad underneath the roller doors and out into the dawn. Before he exited the hangar, he made sure to tuck one of the Glock 19s into his waistband.

Always stay armed. Always stay ready.

'Diego!' Brad called as the pickup screeched to a halt just outside the entrance to the hangar. 'Where have you been?'

'Very sorry, my friend,' the pilot said, clambering out of the vehicle. His accent was thick. 'I was having breakfast.'

'Of course he was,' Clint muttered.

Brad strode up to him. 'I said 0500, Diego. What part of that didn't you understand? This is extremely important.'

'Yes, yes, I understand,' Diego said. 'I understand you, mister. I very sorry. I got held up at cafe.'

'Cafe? What cafes are open at five in the morning?'

'Not many. Just the one I always go. Karma Cafe. Very good food. Fantastic. But I get held up by stranger, wanting to talk. Otherwise, I be on time!'

Brad hesitated. 'What stranger?'

'Ah, it was nothing.'

'Tell us,' Brad said, more insistent. His tone had changed. Less scolding; more wary.

'Man come up. He say, "Hey, Diego!" But I don't know him. But then, maybe I forget him. I no want to offend. I say hey back. He say, "Diego, my friend, what you doing today?" I say I flying tourist into rainforest. Then he run off. Just like that.' Diego clicked his fingers for added effect.

King's heart rate increased instantly. 'Oh, that's not good.'

Brad slammed a closed fist down on the bonnet of Diego's truck, infuriated. 'Why the *fuck* would you tell him what you're doing?'

'I didn't!' Diego yelled. 'You see, I say tourist! I don't say soldier! He does not know.'

'Did you make sure you weren't being followed here?' King demanded.

'I—'

'Answer the question!'

'I don't know. I no pay attention.'

'Diego, did you ever stop to think that you shouldn't go around telling people about top-secret tasks you've been paid handsomely to do?'

'I dunno,' Diego said, flabbergasted. 'You no tell me much. I dunno if it was important!'

'We're probably okay,' King said to Brad. 'Chances are it's nothing.'

Then came the thunderous sound of tearing metal, and the four of them stared across the airfield to see a black four-wheel-drive burst through the flimsy metal gate. It slid momentarily across the grass. Then it revved its engine and powered toward the hangar, heading straight for them.

CHAPTER 6

King didn't act for a split second. He focused hard, staring at the 4WD. It was imperative he caught a glimpse of the number of hostiles. He saw a figure running after the vehicle, attempting to catch it from behind.

The guard at the gate.

The rear window of the 4WD rolled down and a thin man leant out. He clutched some type of assault rifle in his hands. King couldn't make out the exact type from this distance. The assailant let out a quick burst of fire, *rat-a-tat-tat*, and the guard dropped like a rag doll.

'Inside!' King roared.

Brad's instincts kicked in and he reacted fast, wrapping an arm around Clint and tugging him into the hangar. It was the necessary action to jumpstart Clint's movements. He'd been frozen solid, startled by the gunfire. Now he found his feet and bolted inside.

With one swift motion, Diego dropped to the tarmac and rolled under his truck. A practiced move. King wondered if he often found himself in the middle of shootouts. He had no more time to ponder that idea, as a hail of bullets churned up the tarmac all around him. He got one look at the 4WD — now sporting three men hanging out the windows, all brandishing fully automatic weapons — before darting into the hangar, behind cover.

It did not take long to realise what was about to happen. With dawning dread, King let out a shout.

'Clint, to the *side!*'

It was too late. Clint, in his inexperience, had decided to flee in a straight line away from the enemy vehicle. He'd sprinted down the centre of the hangar, toward the cover of the Cessna.

Too far away.

King watched as his back turned to pulp, lit up by a barrage of bullets. He stopped running. Staggered. His head swivelled side to side, eyes wide and bulging. There was nothing anyone could do to save him.

Whether he would have succumbed to those injuries did not matter. The round that punched through the side of his skull finished him off.

It was less graphic than King expected it to be. He'd seen some gruesome injuries during his time in the field. He'd seen men bleed more liquid than he thought could possibly be contained within a human body. The sight was always grisly, and something he attempted to avoid revisiting. The killing round that hit Clint sliced through his head, just above his ear, and pulverised his brain.

He died instantaneously.

King couldn't help but feel relief that the bullet had found its target in the side of his head. Not for any malicious reason. In fact, he felt a stab of sadness as he watched Clint's limp body fall to the concrete. He'd warmed to the analyst. But he knew that if the man hadn't been killed by that shot, he would have bled out slowly, over the course of hours. It would have been accompanied by an unfathomable amount of pain. A quick and painless departure was in all ways preferable. If King had to choose the method of his own death further down the line, a bullet to the brain would be one of the most favourable outcomes.

He withdrew the Glock 19 from his waistband. It was a small pistol. Compact. Designed for concealed carry as well as use in the field. But experience had taught King that the length of a barrel did not change how fast a bullet entered an enemy's head. The Glock 19 was pinpoint accurate, and that was what truly mattered.

Diego had fallen out of his line of sight. He would worry about the pilot later. Brad, on the other hand, was clearly visible. He'd ducked off to the far side of the hangar, putting a corrugated iron wall between himself and the 4WD. Just as

King had done. A clear example of the quick thinking that separated the dead from the living.

'You hear them?' Brad called from across the space.

King nodded. The racket of the growling engine grew closer. 'You think they know we're right here?'

'I can't be sure.'

'My bet is they'll come speeding in. Be ready.'

King let his pulse quicken. The icy determination of imminent combat was upon him. He knew he had less than five seconds before the 4WD came roaring into the hangar.

He closed his eyes for a brief moment. Zoning in.

Now.

As soon as he saw the bonnet of the vehicle pass through the entrance he broke into a full sprint toward it. His timing paid off. As the truck charged into the building the men hanging out each window rotated wildly, desperately searching for targets. It took the two men on the left-hand side a fraction too long to notice King.

That half-second cost them their lives.

He raised the Glock with a rigid arm and squeezed off a single shot. His aim did not falter. Neither did the bullet. A loud discharge echoed off the walls and the man hanging out of the passenger seat jerked back, a red burst coating the matte black paint of the 4WD. Shocked by the sudden turn of events, the man behind him spun his rifle around to face King. He managed to fire two bullets.

Way off.

King felt them whisk past him as his stride quickened. He reached the truck just as it slammed on the brakes, the driver reacting to the now stone-dead passenger. King wound up and swung a well-placed fist at the assailant hanging out of the back seat. Squeezed his shoulder blades. Swung round. Followed through. His knuckles smashed into the man's chin, breaking bone and tearing cartilage in his neck. His head whipped to the side and he slumped back inside the car, instantly unconscious.

The driver panicked. As King assumed he would. Two of his men had been incapacitated in the blink of an eye. King heard the screech of tyres and knew the 4WD was about to take off again.

In one movement he wrenched the door open and threw himself inside the truck.

Fighting for your life at close quarters inside a moving vehicle with two limp bodies in the mix was chaotic, to say the least. King thrived on chaos. It was something his enemies were never used to. But it was something he fully prepared for.

His eyes darted left and right. Assessing. Calculating.

There were two threats. The driver, currently focusing on slamming the accelerator. And the man in the back seat with him, separated by the limp body of his unconscious friend.

'What the—' the thug started.

King planted his feet on the floor and sprung across the man he'd just knocked out. He slammed into the thug, crushing him against the far door. Now the fight raged directly behind the driver. If he had a weapon, it would be difficult to fire a shot under these circumstances.

King wrapped an arm around the thug's throat, taking advantage of the confusion. A glancing blow bounced off the side of his head. It did little to faze him. He locked his hands together and squeezed like a madman. Tensing all the muscles in his forearm, he pulled and wrenched and constricted like his life depended on it.

Which it did.

He'd locked the choke in under the chin, which was disastrous in any street fight. Nine times out of ten it led to unconsciousness. With a man of King's power and explosiveness, half the time it resulted in a crushed larynx, and possibly death.

It didn't take long for the thug to join his comrade in unconsciousness. King felt him go limp, and released him instantly. There was no use wasting time making sure he was dead. For now, he was out of the fight. That was all that mattered.

Now, a new situation appeared. King and the driver were the only two people still conscious. The three bodies surrounding them were either dead, or close to. The driver quickly recognised how the tables had turned. He no longer had the advantage of numbers. He was about to enter combat with the man who had dispatched his three colleagues effortlessly, at the same time battling for control of an enormous motor vehicle. The odds were skewed heavily against him.

'Give up,' King said.

A futile statement. There would be no surrender. He watched the driver stamp down one last time, crushing the accelerator into the footwell. The engine roared and the speedometer spiked. Their surroundings quickened to a blur. The vehicle had already been clocking close to sixty miles an hour. Now it surged forward. One final burst of momentum.

The driver bailed before King could move. One moment he was there, white knuckles clutching the wheel determinedly. Then he reached down, tugged the handle and fell out the open space created by the door swinging open. As he disappeared, King saw what lay ahead. His view had been obscured by the back of the driver's head. Now he saw the far wall of the hangar growing closer, expanding, filling his vision. The car was seconds away from impact.

He felt a pang of shock in his gut. He knew he was in an awkward position. The unconscious thug's body lay splayed across him, pinning him in place. He took a deep breath and exploded into action. Fuelled by a burst of primal energy. The type of strength that only materialised in life-or-death situations. With one hand he threw the man away like a discarded plaything. With the other, he reached sideways. Desperate, manic. Knowing he would be pulverised if he was not out of the car in a second.

Two fingers found the door handle.

He tugged.

It opened.

Using one last surge of movement he dove. Springing off the footwell. Flailing head-first toward the gap.

Halfway out the door the vehicle ploughed into the hangar wall with breathtaking force.

CHAPTER 7

King felt the car crumple around him.

An ear-splitting shriek of tearing metal raged everywhere, from all directions, filling his senses. But he was out. With milliseconds to spare. The edge of the door clipped his ankles. Spun him around in mid-air. Threw him onto the concrete. He landed hard, back-first. Rolled with it. The impact flung him head-over-heels, careering across the concrete. First his upper back, then his shoulder.

Then — just as suddenly as the chaos had started — it stopped.

King tumbled to a halt a safe distance away from the wreck. Before his vision even returned to him his brain frantically sent signals through his limbs, searching for any dire injuries.

No broken bones. Nothing impeding his movement. His tumble-roll had reduced the majority of the force behind the landing. Sure, he would be excruciatingly sore when the adrenalin wore off. Soft tissue damage was inevitable. Half his body would be bruised.

Right now, that was inconsequential.

There was still one hostile alive.

The corrugated iron wall had taken just as much damage as the 4WD. It was thick material, but the collision had demolished much of its form. The car itself was a battered mess, its bonnet smoking, glass strewn everywhere. Ten feet away, the driver lay on the concrete. Shell-shocked from the landing.

He'd hit the concrete violently, much harder than King had.

King would capitalise on his inability to act.

He sprung to his feet, ignoring the nerve endings across his body screaming for him to rest. Slowly, tentatively, the driver rose too.

In unison, they both saw it.

The Glock 19 had been flung from the wreck, thrown out of King's hands as he dove to safety. It lay in the space between them. Still spinning slowly on its side.

The driver recognised the importance of the gun, and charged at it.

King was three steps ahead.

In one motion he reached down and scooped the weapon off the ground. His finger slid into the trigger guard. He took another bounding step toward the driver and levelled the gun.

Then the driver's actions took him by surprise. Clearly a trained mercenary, the man reached out and wrapped his hands around the gun with surprising accuracy and power. King felt it slipping from his grip as he depressed the trigger. A single round spat from the barrel and hit the man squarely in the centre of the chest, accompanied by the vicious noise of steel sinking through bone.

The driver would succumb to his wounds, that was for sure.

But that meant nothing, for now he had control of the Glock.

'Gun!' a voice roared from behind them.

King spun to see Brad storming across the hangar floor. The SCAR assault rifle from the duffel bag sat on his shoulder. He peered down the sights, aim locked directly on the driver.

King stood in between them.

He flung himself out of the way, arcing sideways through the air. He hit the ground hard and came to a skidding halt. Just in time to see events unfold.

Brad fired a burst from the rifle. His aim rang true. Three rounds tore up the driver's chest, tearing his jacket to shreds. One of them hit his vital organs. King saw his eyes glaze over.

Then the driver fell to his knees, raised the Glock and spat out a final, desperate shot. The reverberation echoed off the walls. Finally, there was silence.

King breathed a sigh of relief and turned to thank Brad on coming to his rescue.

Which he found would be impossible.

Brad sported a cylindrical bullet hole in his temple. An instantly fatal shot. The life in his eyes had already died out. King watched the limp body slump to the concrete. He took a moment to process the sight.

He was the last man alive in the warehouse.

He let his head fall back against the concrete, sucking in air, recovering from the brutal series of events. The only sound came from the wind slicing through the entrance and whistling around the empty hangar. He closed his eyes and let the calm of the aftermath wash over him.

'This is fucked,' he whispered, effectively summarising what had just occurred.

The operation had been torn apart before it was even supposed to begin.

CHAPTER 8

He heard Diego stumble into the hangar not long after. He kept his eyes closed, reeling from the close call.

'Oh my god,' the pilot exclaimed.

'I'm alive, Diego,' King shouted.

He opened his eyes to see Diego jolt, startled by the sound of a man he'd thought to be dead. He looked around. Brad and the driver lay opposite each other, face-down in pools of their own blood. The body of one of the passengers hung half out the window of the obliterated 4WD. Near the Cessna, Clint's body slumped motionless.

'Jesus Christ,' Diego said. 'What the — oh my god.' He struggled to form a coherent sentence. The man was clearly in a considerable state of shock.

Understandably, King thought. With no prior combat experience, the scene he gazed upon would be far too bizarre to process. It was time to relay clear, concise instructions to Diego until they were out of this mess.

King rose off the floor and laid a hand on the man's shoulder.

'My name is Jason King,' he said, slowly and calmly. 'I didn't get a chance to introduce myself earlier. I'm a soldier. A very good one. I'm going to get you to safety, okay?'

'Okay.' Diego remained unable to peel his eyes away from the bodies strewn across the hangar.

'Look at me, Diego.'

The pilot glanced briefly in his general direction.

'We need to go through with the plan,' King said. 'Do you hear me?'

'Uh...' he said, his gaze flittering from body to body. 'I dunno, mister.'

'Everyone who came for us is dead. The gang in the jungle will have no idea that we're still on our way. All you need to do is follow exactly what I tell you. As soon as I'm out of your plane, you can fly back here, contact the authorities and forget this whole thing ever happened. Our command will take care of you. I promise.'

Diego's lips remained firmly sealed. King didn't know if he would get a response.

'Did you hear me?'

Diego nodded.

'Will you do what I say?'

Another nod.

'Do you think you can still fly the Cessna?'

'Yes,' Diego said. 'I fly plane for many years. Can do it with eyes shut.'

'That's good, Diego. The faster we do this, the faster you can get back home. Would you like that?'

Diego nodded again. 'They all dead, King.'

'I know.'

'You kill them?'

'I killed all the men in the truck. Clint and Brad didn't make it.'

'I see dead body before,' Diego said. 'But never this many. Never this much blood.'

'Let's get out of here. Nothing else to see.'

'Are you okay?'

'I'll be fine. But there's some people in the jungle who won't be unless we go right now. It's up to me to extract them. You got that?'

'I got it. Let's go.'

King led him to the small aircraft in the centre of the hangar and helped him into the pilot's seat. As Diego preoccupied himself firing up the engine, he went back to Brad and plied the SCAR from his dead hands. He would no longer be needing it. King looked at the trestles tables. Sure enough, everything on their surface had been torn to shreds by gunfire.

The satellite phones lay in pieces on the concrete floor. Completely ruined.

No backup.

His skin grew cold and he gulped, suddenly anxious, but it would do no good to let it show. Diego was dealing with enough already. He didn't need to see a special forces soldier scared out of his mind.

Before King left, he stopped and glanced back at Brad. The man's face sported the expression of steely determination, still frozen from his last moments. No surprise. No fear. He had never known his fate.

King knelt down and rested a hand on Brad's vest, spending one final moment with the corpse. Then he jogged back to the tables, stuffed the SCAR into the duffel bag, zipped it up, threw it into the plane alongside the parachute container and clambered in through the open fuselage door.

'Ready?' he said to Diego.

'Ready.'

The pilot thumbed a button and the single propellor at the front of the plane whined into life, deafeningly loud. The drone of the engine drowned out all other sound. If King shouted, nothing would be heard.

He reached up and swung the door shut, sealing the interior in relative silence. Now there was nothing but a cluster of nervous energy inside the plane. A small, claustrophobic tin can, which he would soon be exiting at 14,000 feet. After all the death he had just witnessed, the jump seemed rather inconsequential.

'How will I explain if police find this before I return?' Diego said softly, his voice barely audible above the shuddering fuselage.

'I know people so high up the ranks they could make this disappear in an instant,' King said. 'You'll be safe. I swear.'

Silence.

'Do you know where you're going?' King said.

Diego nodded. 'Your friends give me co-ordinates.'

'Just get me there. I'll handle the rest.'

As he sat on the floor of the tiny plane and felt the vertigo in his stomach as it lifted off the runway, the gravity of the situation began to dawn on him. Brad and Clint were his only form of backup. He had no way out of the rainforest after he entered it, save for a hundred mile hike. No form of communications with his superiors in the government. The plan had been shoddy to begin with, even before the clusterfuck that had just unfolded.

His only hope at making it out alive was to steal communications equipment off one of the Phantoms. The men at the facility had to have some method of contacting their friends in Iquitos. King would find that method, no matter how many bodies he had to pile up to do so.

The three hostages needed him. He would do everything in his power to get them out.

He let his back rest against the wall behind him and felt the light aircraft shudder and shake in the wind. He was thirty minutes away from falling into the middle of the rainforest, with limited supplies, no backup, no real knowledge of what he would be facing, or where they were located.

But he was alone.

That was all that mattered. King could do things by himself that entire armies could not achieve. The circumstances did not matter. He was the only one responsible for his survival, and that was just the way he liked it.

CHAPTER 9

Back over the Amazon Rainforest...

As he stepped off the plane half an hour later, the fear instantly dissipated. It wasn't the act itself that scared King. It was the build up. When he opened that door and dove out into thin air with the wind pummelling him from all sides, there was no time to think about anything other than action. The nerves remained. His pulse stayed high. But the sensory overload meant he felt none of those things.

Usually, skydiving was beautiful. King had only done it recreationally a handful of times. He spent the majority of the time in freefall racing toward hostile forces looking to violently murder him. It didn't give him much time to focus on the pleasantries of the experience.

For a while it felt like he was floating. With nothing around him for 14,000 feet, there was nothing to compare his speed to. No way to gauge it. He fell at over one hundred and twenty miles an hour, but it was hard to tell that there was any movement at all.

The wind battered him relentlessly but that was the only noticeable factor. King held his stable position, arching his back and spreading his arms wide. It was a difficult position to control. The duffel bag around his mid-section plus his one-hundred kilogram frame combined to form a significant amount of weight under canopy. A heavy duty parachute had been required to handle his bulk.

It meant he fell like a bullet.

For a moment he admired the view. From this high up the jungle was a sight to behold. Endless plains of green, spanning as far as the eye could see. All lush and serene. He soaked it all in. He knew it wouldn't last.

Sixty seconds from now, there would be nothing to admire.

Survival and completion of the mission would be the only things on his mind when he landed.

It didn't take long for the ground to grow dangerously close. One second the rainforest was nothing but a tiny map far below. The next, it was right there. He began to make out individual trees.

He had to pull off an extremely low opening. Otherwise, his chances of detection would shoot through the roof.

He waited until just before his life fell into endangered territory, then reached back and yanked the ripcord from its position at the bottom of the container.

Nothing happened.

King didn't panic. There was always a delay. A second of hesitation as the canopy billowed from the container. Most men would be certain of their impending death. The rainforest was less than a thousand feet below him. It felt like he would impact at any moment.

Calm, he told himself.

Then the chute caught the wind. A sudden jerk on his shoulder straps. The resounding *whump* of a fully opened canopy. He slowed in an instant.

Just in time.

The treetops were so near his feet he could almost kick them. It was the closest he had ever cut an opening. Another second's hesitation and he would have been skewered on the branches. Preferably killed instantly. Worse case scenario: he would have bled out over the course of the day.

Now that he was alive, the hard part began.

King braced for impact.

He had a beat or two before he crashed into the trees at close to thirty miles an hour. He reached up and snatched the toggles on either side of his head. Usually they were used for steering.

There was no time to steer.

King yanked down hard on both toggles. Each side of the canopy bent toward him, effectively slowing him down. The move was known as 'flaring'. It was used by all skydivers to reduce their speed before touching down. Most skydivers touched down on flat ground though.

'Fuck,' King muttered under his breath, preparing for what came next.

He slammed into a palm tree chest-first. Its large drooping fronds took away a little of the force behind the impact, but the hit still knocked the breath from his lungs. He spiralled away from the tree, now inside the rainforest. Branches tore at his khaki gear. He spun. Unsure which way was up, which way was down. Then a violent tug at his shoulders.

And he stopped.

He looked up. The canopy had caught on the branches and fronds above his head, severely entangled. There would be no salvaging the parachute. It was a miracle it hadn't been torn to shreds already. King now dangled from the container's straps, looping over his shoulders like a backpack. The weight of his gear threatened to cause significant problems. He heard the string lines of the parachute straining, threatening to give. They would snap if he didn't act.

He took a second to get his bearings. The rainforest floor was as he expected. Dense and inhospitable. It would be difficult terrain to traverse. Foliage and overgrowth covered everything.

His current situation was far more precarious. A distance of at least twenty feet separated him from the ground. The vegetation was widespread, but it would not be enough to save him from broken limbs if he fell. Any serious injury in these parts would be a death sentence.

First he unclipped the duffel bag from his chest, letting it fall. There was significant weight in the bag and it made a hollow *thud* as it hit the ground below. King paused, slowly rotating in his harness.

Silence.

No sounds came from the jungle. Not even the chattering of wildlife. He assumed the parachute crash had caused enough commotion to scare off any animals in the vicinity. In the distance, he heard the exotic call of a native bird. But no signs of human activity. Nothing to signal he had been spotted.

Time to move.

He undid the strap around his waist. Then slowly and tentatively extracted one arm from the harness. The move swung him round. He shot his free arm around and snatched hold of the pack.

Now with both hands wrapped around the container's straps, he hung suspended in the air, both feet dangling. There was nowhere to go but up. Breathing heavily with exertion he pulled himself up and snatched hold of one of the string lines connecting the canopy to the container. With the extra weight of the duffel bag gone, the thin lines managed to support his weight.

Barely.

Although designed to hold a man in a harness, there were more than twenty of them. With two in each hand, the uneven distribution of the weight threatened to tear the canopy if he wasn't careful. He began to slowly shimmy up the lines, attempting to spread his bulk out as evenly as possible.

'This isn't good,' he whispered, staring up at the canopy.

It started to give. A tear in the fabric began to widen. It threatened to split the entire thing in half, sending him tumbling down to injury. He had to do something to avoid that situation before he wound up left for dead in the middle of the jungle.

A sturdy branch jutted out of a tree trunk a few feet above his head. He couldn't reach it yet. But it was his best shot at survival.

He threw caution to the wind and lurched upward. Grabbing as many of the string lines as possible. Reaching as high as he could. As he hurried, the canopy tore, accompanied by the sound of ripping fabric. One final burst and he was within touching distance of the branch.

As he pulled on the string lines one last time they came down, sending a pang of shock through his chest. For a single terrifying moment he hung suspended in the air. Holding onto nothing. Milliseconds from falling.

Then he shot his hand out and wrapped three fingers around the branch.

CHAPTER 10

The canopy finished tearing in half. It cascaded to the forest floor below as King hung, breathless and shocked, still nowhere near safety. It would be a long trek down.

He began his journey, making slow deliberate movements. Any slip-up now would spell serious trouble. First he swung hand-over-hand along the branch. Not recklessly and spectacularly like Tarzan. But very carefully, and very hesitantly. Style points meant nothing out here.

He shimmied to where the branch met the trunk, and planned his next move. The tree was tall but its trunk was disproportionately thin. Still wider than a man, but small enough so he could wrap his arms around its girth and lock down a proper grip. He splayed his legs and arms out wide, feeling the rough bark against his fingertips. It would suffice.

He inched toward the ground. Each move was delicate, measured, cautious. First he scraped his all-weather boots down the trunk, then loosened the tension in his hands and dragged them in the same direction. He took care not to take the skin off his palms as he manoeuvred his way down. He would need fresh hands when he made it to the bottom.

The knot in his gut began to subside as he made it within fifteen feet of the ground. Any fall from this distance would hurt, but would avoid the disastrous ramifications of serious injury.

He touched down on solid ground roughly two minutes after landing in the trees. If not for the subconscious timer in his head that invariably ticked away at all hours of the day, he would have thought he'd spent hours up there. He knew most sane men would fear the thought of dying at the hands of mercenaries more than sustaining a fall-related injury in the rainforest.

But most men did not have the experience that King did. He knew which would be less painful. And it wasn't the wrong end of a bullet.

The duffel had landed in the shallow space between two logs covered in moss. He zigzagged around at least a dozen different plants to retrieve it. The sheer volume of undergrowth covering everything was stifling. King already felt the humidity eating away at him. Under his khakis, droplets of sweat trickled down his skin. It was uncomfortable as all hell, but comfortability sat at the bottom of his current list of priorities.

First — get his bearings.

He slung the duffel over one shoulder, wiped sweat off his brow and looked around. Three directions held nothing but endless rows of trees, clustered sporadically, wrapped in various ferns and plants. These ways barred easy travel. But to his left, King saw a break in the trees up ahead. The sound of running water sounded just past the break.

A river.

It would be the first step in locating the Phantoms' facility. He set off at a brisk pace. As brisk as one could manage in the conditions. Each footfall had to be carefully placed. He had to ensure he didn't turn his ankle and incapacitate himself before he even found the hostiles.

The sounds of the jungle were far different to anything he'd ever heard before. As the commotion of his crash-landing faded into obscurity, the catcalls of birds and shrieks of animals began to creep back into the surroundings. King recalled some vague fact he'd heard about the Amazon Rainforest holding hundreds of different bird species. He wasn't sure exactly how many. But he heard every single one of them as he trekked. Their calls ranged from short, sharp chirps to long drawn-out hoots, each with their own personality and resonance.

He stopped concentrating on the birds when he stepped out onto the riverbank and made direct eye contact with two men holding automatic weapons.

CHAPTER 11

No one said a word. King's pulse leapt through the roof.

He'd emerged from between two trees to see a murky river snaking away to the left and the right, flowing fast. The banks were built up with a mixture of churned dirt and washed-up sticks. The two men stood in front of a cluster of four rickety boats, each with a sizeable outboard motor on the back.

He watched as they both went through a period of momentary confusion, the type of emotion that pops up when you come face-to-face with what appears to be a soldier in territory you believed to be uninhabited. They looked similar. Olive skin, lean muscular builds, dirty complexions. Both clutched battered and rusty Kalashnikov AK-74s. And both had the same insignia branded on their upper arms. A ghastly skull, forged from their burnt skin.

A phantom.

One man had long straggly hair and wore a combat vest over his bare torso, which was slick with sweat. The other kept his hair short, cut close to the skull. He wore a tattered singlet, exuding confidence. Just from his demeanour, he appeared to be the dominant member of the pair. He stood slightly taller. His body language was more confident. His shoulders straighter. His reaction to the confrontation less panicked.

So King shot him first.

He reached down and ripped the Glock 19 out of its holster at his waist in one motion. Levelled it. Fired a round into the short-haired man's skull before the other guy could blink. There was no blood, no guts, no graphic explosion of gore. Just a well-placed shot that crumpled the gangster, killing him instantly.

The sound of the Glock's report shook the long-haired guy into action. He brought the barrel of his AK-74 up, his aim searching. King recognised he was a second away from death and ducked behind one of the thick palm trees lining the shore.

He felt the reverberations in the trunk as bullets tore into the wood on the other side. They whisked all around him, slicing through fronds and leaves to his left and right. Crouching behind cover, he couldn't help but smile. The man shooting at him was unaccustomed to combat. He'd spent a significant length of time in the middle of the Amazon Rainforest, armed to the teeth with nothing to fight against. When action finally struck, he was thoroughly unprepared. King knew within seconds his magazine would run dry. Overcompensating on his aggression would be his downfall.

Click.

There it was. The oppressing hail of gunfire stopped at once.

King paused for a beat, making sure the man was in the process of reloading by the time he stepped out. He heard nothing. It was time.

He brought the Glock up to shoulder height, arm stretched out rigid, and rounded the tree.

No-one there.

It took him by surprise. It wasn't often that he miscalculated a situation. He'd fully expected the man to be standing in the exact place he'd last seen him, fumbling with a fresh magazine in the bottom of his Kalashnikov. Instead he saw nothing. An empty river bank. The trees on the other side of the river, rustling softly in the breeze. And at the very edge of his vision, a leg disappearing into the jungle just a dozen feet ahead.

He heard the sounds of branches and undergrowth snapping, rustling, shifting. Sounds that weren't part of the natural atmosphere of the rainforest. He took a moment to appreciate the quick thinking of the mercenary.

King had underestimated him, and he'd capitalised on the situation. He'd run out of bullets and instantly run into the jungle, protected from returning fire by dense foliage. King didn't know how close the facility was. For all he knew, if he didn't kill the man, he would be surrounded by dozens of hostiles within minutes. He couldn't let that happen.

Desperation got the better of him. Without control of the situation, King knew he had to act recklessly in order to swing the advantage in his favour. If he played it safe he would be dead in no time.

Massive instantaneous action was the only answer.

He dropped the duffel onto the forest floor and broke into a sprint, legs pumping like pistons. He didn't care if he turned an ankle anymore. There were far greater things to worry about. The entire operation would be compromised if news was raised of his arrival. His main advantage was the fact that he was a ghost, and would be able to creep around the outskirts of the compound without a chance of detection. Scouting, planning, waiting for the perfect time to strike.

That plan would shortly be ruined.

So he threw caution to the wind and powered through the foliage, smashing aside low-hanging fronds and leaping obstacles dotting the ground. He determined his path by rough estimation. In parts of the jungle where the vegetation was this dense, seeing more than a few feet ahead was impossible. The rainforest obscured everything. King hoped he was heading in the right direction. He also hoped he could find his way back to the duffel bag later. It would have been better to bring it with him, but it was too heavy. Too cumbersome. With it on his back, he would never find the man.

It turned out he need not have worried.

He burst through a particularly hefty palm leaf, brushing it aside, and instantly felt a crushing blow in his mid-section. He lost his footing and sprawled against a log, careering backward. It slammed the breath from his lungs and he rolled aside, wheezing. It took him longer than it should have to realise he'd been tackled.

The mercenary had waited for King to come charging out. Then he had charged in return. And it had worked.

King knew he'd lost the upper hand. The sudden impact sent the Glock in his hand spinning away, lost in the undergrowth.

'Motherfucker,' he spat at the mercenary.

The man smiled, revealing stained yellow teeth. Clearly there was a shortage of dental care in the Amazon Rainforest.

'You're dead,' he said, confident. He bent down to pick up the AK-74 he'd left on the ground.

King scrambled to his feet, took a single leaping bound and launched. Revoking all care for his body. He would land hard, and it would be painful. But it didn't matter. At least he wouldn't be torn apart by Russian steel-core bullets.

He raised both legs and lashed out, double-footed, vicious. Putting all two hundred pounds of his bulk behind the kick. His boots struck the mercenary square in the solar plexus, transferring force through his hips to his knees to his feet to the guy's torso. The mercenary let out an audible wheeze, clearly stunned by the force of the attack. He released his hold on the rifle as he skidded off his feet. He landed hard on his rear and his head bounced off a tree trunk, dazing him momentarily.

King landed with equally painful results.

He'd thrown himself almost horizontal with the attack and as a result came down on the small of his back on uneven ground. A white hot burst of pain flashed up his spine and for a moment he feared a serious injury. Two seconds later, he tested his movement and found he was okay.

It just hurt like hell.

He'd thrown the kick with reckless abandon but it had done its job. Guns were out of the equation. The Kalashnikov had spiralled away into the shrubs, rendered useless. It wouldn't be found without a search. There was no way King would give the man time for one.

They rose simultaneously. King knew he had the upper hand now. He had an extra fifty pounds on the guy, at least. There were weight classes in professional combat sports for a reason. No matter how much of a skill gap, eventually it reached a point where the bigger man would always have the advantage. Luckily, King had both the skill, speed and size advantage over most men on the planet.

The man used shaking hands to draw a knife from a leather sheath at his waist. It was a coarse, serrated thing. Useful for hacking through vegetation. It wouldn't help him now.

King faked a jab low then threw a head kick in a scything arc. He opened up his hips and turned at the waist and pivoted on his left heel and followed through, whipping his boot through the air with the force of a freight train. A move practiced on heavy bags thousands upon thousands of times, whether deep in the bowels of a United States government facility or in the small mixed martial arts gyms he frequented in his off time.

The countless hours he spent in solitude paid off.

The kick felt smooth. So well-practiced that it became something effortless, like an extension of himself. He recalled taking a heavy bag off its hinges with a similar kick earlier this year, tearing a large chunk of plaster out of the roof with it.

The man in front of him had been sold by the fake, and as a result his face was in the exact position King wanted it. The top of his foot connected with the mercenary's jaw in just the right place. He heard delicate bones shatter and the man collapsed into the undergrowth, knocked unconscious by the kick. Simple as that. No bloody brawl, no battle for survival. Just a single well-placed, well-executed strike. It took nothing more. Real life was very different to the movies. The brain was a fragile thing, and concussions could be exploited if one knew the perfect place to hit.

The two hostiles were out of the equation. For now, he was safe.

CHAPTER 12

King took a deep breath and let the heat of combat wash off him. His heart rate slowed. He had trained it to do so. The action was over and it was time to conserve his energy. The adrenalin of life-or-death confrontations would exhaust him if he let it drag on any longer than was needed.

He stepped over to the last place he had seen the Kalashnikov fall. Brushed aside a mass of vegetation. Saw the glint of an automatic weapon, resting against the stalk of a plant. He bent down and scooped up the AK-74. It was a thing of beauty, exactly what he looked for in a gun. It didn't matter what the conditions were. The rifle would always shoot. In rain, in mud, in snow, in the desert. No matter what, it would work.

King walked back to the unconscious man. Paused for a moment. Ejected the magazine and checked it. It was full. He couldn't help but be impressed. The mercenary had reloaded the rifle while sprinting away from King. A level-headed move, that hadn't helped him in the end. King aimed the

Kalashnikov and fired a single bullet through the sleeping man's skull.

He felt no emotion. This man would have skewered him with his serrated knife given the opportunity. Either finished him off there and then or let him bleed out in the jungle. If King showed him mercy and left him unconscious, he would no doubt die a slow painful death when he came to, impaired by the concussion and out of food and water. Being shot while asleep would be the most pain-free way to go. There was little mercy out here in operations like these, but King at least gave the man that. There was no need to add unnecessary pain and trauma. The head kick had taken him by surprise, so he had never seen his death coming.

Much like Brad.

King stopped and listened. He counted two unsuppressed shots in the last few minutes, from his Glock and the Kalashnikov. On top of that, the mercenary had fired a clip of at least fourteen bullets in his general direction back on the riverbank. If the Phantoms' facility was close, alarms would already have been raised. Fully-armed men would be heading for him already. He probably wouldn't stand a chance.

Nothing. No sound of yelling, or movement, or anything of the sort. The compound was out of earshot. So far, nothing had changed.

Then he looked down at the dead man's body and saw a radio attached to his belt. A crappy old digital device with a short stocky antenna, all black, the frequency listed on the tiny screen. A small red light flashed on the side of it. He looked at the light and felt his gut tighten. He heard a brief crackle of static.

Shit, he thought.

The radio was in contact with someone. While running, the mercenary had switched it on. Someone at the compound had heard the commotion that had just transpired.

He bent down and extracted the device from the belt. Picked it up. Raised it to his ear. Sure enough, the distinct sound of white noise filtered through the tiny speaker. Someone was listening. King didn't say a word.

'Who are you?'

The voice came from the radio. Short, sharp, deep. In English, but heavily accented. Filled with menace and hostility. King was intruding on the territory of some dangerous, powerful people. They would be cruel if they caught him. They would be unrelenting. He could hear it in the voice. They had no idea who he was, but he was a threat, and he would be torn apart if they got their hands on him.

He smashed the radio against the nearest tree trunk, breaking it into pieces. Shards of plastic cascaded to the forest floor. The static abruptly ceased. But it was a futile effort, far too late. A move only enacted out of anger. The compound was onto him. They knew there was a hostile, somewhere in the jungle. That gave them an infinitely larger advantage.

King stood very still, contemplating just how exactly he would succeed when a force of heavily armed drug dealers knew someone was heading straight for them.

Short answer: he wouldn't. Not without a healthy dose of luck. Nevertheless, there were no other options. The only way back to civilisation involved storming the compound. Without a satellite phone or radio or any other means of communication, he would be stranded out here until command sorted out the mess the operation had become. His involvement was highly classified as it was; only a handful of Pentagon defence chiefs knew he was assigned to the task. The ground forces reaching Iquitos in the coming hours would be oblivious to the fact that he had been inserted into the situation.

First step was to locate the facility. King knew it was concealed from the air, under cover of branches. He knew it was somewhere nearby. That about covered the extent of his prior knowledge. Three quarters of the rainforest was concealed from any prying eyes above, so this information did little to assist.

He assumed the man he'd just killed had been heading back to base. In his reactionary state, he would have fled toward what was familiar before deciding to lay in wait and ambush King. King decided he would continue in that general direction.

First he discarded the AK-74 into the bushes and retrieved his Glock. The Kalashnikov was an effective, reliable weapon, yet ultimately rudimentary. King's gear far outclassed the equipment wielded by the Phantoms. Before any further action, he knew he would need to retrieve his duffel. It had everything he needed. Without it, he was as good as dead.

It took ten minutes to locate. King did not let himself grow panicked. He quickly squashed down the fear in his gut. Irrational panic would do nothing but hinder his progress. He returned to the shore, found the tree riddled with bullets and combed through the surrounding vegetation with meticulous attention to detail. Eventually he found the bag, concealed under a cluster of ferns. He slung it back over his shoulder and headed north, the last direction the second mercenary had headed.

The time approached noon. Before returning to the claustrophobic conditions of the rainforest, King stared up at the sun and took a deep breath, inhaling the scent of the river. The sun's rays beat down on him, drawing sweat from his pores, but he didn't care. He revelled in the moment of calm before what he knew would be a particularly violent and chaotic storm.

Then he strode up the riverbank and ducked back into the jungle.

CHAPTER 13

It wasn't long before he heard man-made sounds in the distance. They were faint, on the very edge of what was audible, but nevertheless they didn't align with the natural atmosphere of the rainforest. Muffled voices, far off. Definitely human.

King was onto them.

A brief flash of relief passed over him. It wasn't much of an achievement. He was probably heading for certain death, toward a compound full of drug gangsters armed to the teeth and ready for a firefight. But it was progress, and finding the facility was preferable to trekking through the rainforest for hours with nothing to show for it.

Before he moved in, he reached into the duffel and withdrew a weatherproof water canister. He'd filled it up from a pool of rainwater that had gathered inside a large frond leaf. He had passed the leaf ten minutes earlier, and dropped a couple of water purification tablets into the bottle as he'd filled it. The tablets were top of the line, not for sale on the general market, mainly because of their exorbitant production cost. They were used exclusively by special forces who found themselves in remote hazardous regions. King wasn't sure of the technicalities, but he knew they exterminated anything dangerous within five minutes. He just used what was given to him.

He raised the canister to his lips and took a long drink. It tasted fine. Bearable, which was all that mattered. He didn't care for pleasantries. Nothing out here mattered except the mission.

King made sure the duffel was fastened tight to his back, then dropped to the rainforest floor and began to crawl through the undergrowth. It dirtied his clothes and face within seconds. Once again, nothing but unpleasant. Far more important things to worry about. But he knew he would happen upon the facility any moment, and it would be wise to stay hidden from prying eyes.

Slowly, the muffled voices grew louder. They turned to audible phrases, spoken in Spanish. King knew enough of the language to pick up the gist of conversation. Multiple hostiles, all conversing across a fair distance. Loud enough that King could hear their voices carry from a few dozen feet away.

'Mabaya said there's a guy out there in the jungle. He killed Manuel and Alois.'

'You don't know that. You're talking shit. They'll be back.'

'Mabaya heard it on the radio.'

'You don't know anything.'

'He's gonna kill the hostages.'

'Who, the guy out there?'

'No. Mabaya.'

'Good. Fuck them. American pigs.'

Mabaya ... that was Swahili for "monster". King noted that he sounded like the man in charge. They spoke of Mabaya as if he possessed a level of authority greater than theirs. It was subtle, but noticeable.

King shuffled into position and slowly transitioned into a crouch, making sure not to make any sudden movements. Avoiding detection was paramount. He rose a fraction of a hair above the ferns. Narrowed his vision. Took a long look at what he could see.

The drug manufacturing facility lay ahead. It was still far enough in the distance to give the hostiles no chance of spotting him. To them he was an unnoticeable speck amongst the dense foliage. But he could see the layout, which he spent valuable time memorising.

The main building was a long low structure made of corrugated iron sheeting, much like a smaller version of the hangar King had spent the previous night in. It looked shoddy, put together hastily. He realised it probably had been.

There was no way to ensure quality this deep into uncharted territory. Concrete trucks or any other form of construction equipment would be impossible to transport to these parts. All supplies would have been brought in by boat. He guessed a compound in the middle of inhospitable rainforest wouldn't prioritise security from enemy forces during its construction. Its builders would not have considered a fully-armed special forces soldier locating and approaching it with the intention of infiltration.

The main building lay in the centre of a small man-made clearing, carefully selected to provide cover from prying eyes. It was clear that vegetation had been removed in order to fit the structure, yet it still remained shrouded in shadow from the enormous drooping palm fronds of the surrounding trees. The fronds formed a sort of ceiling, a canopy above the warehouse. Natural light filtered through a dozen different gaps in the canopy. The result was somewhat eerie. The conditions accentuated shadows while still keeping the area reasonably well-lit.

The main building where King assumed the heroin and cocaine and other narcotics were produced had a cluster of adjoining huts near one end. These were randomly interspersed, made of flimsy wood and sporting thatched roofs. Living quarters. He wondered how they remained standing through the downpours of the wet season.

Six men currently patrolled the space in between the complex and the jungle. A small patch of empty ground, covered in moss and leaves. They shuffled back and forth, still talking. Agitated. Dressed in similar kit to the two men he'd killed near the riverbank. All holding similar weapons. From this distance he had trouble recognising the exact make, but all their rifles looked like Kalashnikovs. Reliable and deadly.

A door connected to the main structure burst open. Out strode a man. His complexion was darker than the rest. He was African, and even from a few dozen feet away his build looked solid. Taller than the rest of the men, he wore a sleeveless vest revealing muscular arms bulging with veins and large hands with thick fingers. Good for fighting. His head was shaved bald.

'Mabaya,' one of the men said in Spanish. 'What's going on?'

'I should ask the same question,' Mabaya said, his deep voice resonating. King instantly recognised it. It was the same voice behind the camera in the hostage video. 'We have a hostile watching us, and you useless fucks are standing around doing nothing.'

King's pulse quickened.

'How do you—'

'He is watching. Trust me. I heard him on the radio kill Alois. Slimy fucker. I know what he's here for.'

'The hostages?'

Mabaya nodded. 'Let's make this tricky for him.'

He stepped back inside. King watched as the men outside shuffled restlessly. They were nervous. This was a foreign situation to them.

Within a minute Mabaya returned.

This time dragging a man by the collar.

The guy's face sported dried blood and several bruises. He was also bald, dressed in a dirty security guard's uniform. King knew who it was. With a sinking suspicion in his gut of what was about to unfold, he witnessed Mabaya drag the ex-soldier Roman Woodford into the middle of the clearing. Visible from all directions to anyone watching from the jungle.

'*American!*' Mabaya roared, switching to English. It reverberated off the trees. 'See this man? Five seconds before I kill him! Five seconds! You show yourself!'

King didn't move. If he gave himself up, they would all be executed. The most likely result of this operation anyway, but one he would strive to avoid. He wasn't sure if Mabaya was bluffing. Many times, he'd watched volatile enemies make bold claims. They rarely followed through. Executing hostages removed the valuable advantage of possessing a safeguard to attack.

'*Four seconds!*'

Mabaya didn't stutter. He stayed supremely confident. Unwavering in his tone.

'*Three!*'

Still no sign of hesitation. A shadow of doubt crept into King's mind. Woodford was on his knees, motionless, staring at the ground. His expression was steely, but beaten. There was no fight he could put up without being shot to pieces. His face sported the saddening look of reserved acceptance.

'*Two!*'

King could do nothing. Revealing his location would result in certain death for him and all three of the hostages. He pictured the young kid Norton's face right before the Phantoms executed him. It sent a shiver down his spine.

'*One!*'

No turning back. What happened next would reveal the situation at stake.

The situation proved to be catastrophic.

King watched in silent horror as Mabaya slid a large machete from a holster at his waist and swung it fast and hard through the air. A downward scything motion. It entered Woodford's neck in just the right place.

Thunk.

Blood arced from the wound in three or four separate locations, spurting to the clearing floor. Woodford's eyes glazed over instantly. Mabaya was a powerful man. The blow had almost taken Woodford's head clean off. King clenched his fists and screamed internally as he witnessed the man collapse, all tension gone from his limbs.

Unquestionably dead.

Just like that.

'You see!' Mabaya roared, even louder than before. King could see the adrenalin in his expression, twisted and leering and full of energy. Murdering a man in cold blood would do that. 'I do not fuck around! American, you have until sunset to show up here. Or I'll kill the boy and the woman. Much more slowly. Much more painfully. Your choice!'

King could not shake the feeling that the operation was already irreversibly fucked.

CHAPTER 14

Of the seven Phantoms outside the building, three walked inside with Mabaya. The other four held their positions, peering in different directions. Looking for any sign of movement in the trees. Woodford's corpse remained on the clearing floor, blood pooling around his upper body.

King quickly reconsidered his next move. With Woodford's death, his last hope of finding an ally with combat experience had also vanished. Jodi Burns and Ben Norton were somewhere inside the complex, no doubt guarded by several men at a time. There would be no easy way to them, save an all-out assault.

And that was a scenario he was entirely unprepared for.

He had no intel on the facility. It remained unclear how many people were in the compound. So far he had seen seven, but it was a large structure. He saw living quarters for at least twenty individuals. On top of this, everyone was ready for action. His element of surprise had disappeared following the confrontation on the riverbank.

It was time to retreat. At least for an hour or two. A difficult decision given the circumstances, but really the only viable option given the recent turn of events. He would have to give the Phantoms' enough time to drop their guard. Surveillance was a tough slog of an activity. Even on his missions, King had trouble keeping watch for hours at a time. Staying at a high enough level of alertness to detect all unnatural activity took practice and immense patience. He predicted these men didn't have the skills necessary. After a while, they would grow tired. Their eyes would get sore. And then King would return and attack ruthlessly, when they least expected it.

He sprawled down to the rainforest floor once again and began to head away from the facility. Right now, the guards would be on their highest level of alertness, still jacked up on nervous energy after witnessing a murder. There was nothing to be done now. King had to let that energy dissipate.

When he was far enough away from the compound to break the line of sight, he got to his feet. His khakis were covered in mud and leaves. They clung to his skin, held there by sweat. Less than ideal conditions.

The rainforest looked the same for the next two hundred feet. He walked in a straight line away from the compound so that it would be easy to find his way back. Before long, the river materialised up ahead. He heard it before he saw it; the soft sound of running water. In these parts, it provided a brief moment of tranquility. King saw slivers of the riverbank ahead through gaps in the trees. It was further upstream than where he had come face-to-face with the two mercenaries. He could tell that much. That meant he was much closer to the compound. He would have to be cautious not to make excess noise.

He scouted the area for a minute, trying to find a suitable location to store his gear. It was important for the spot to be sheltered from prying eyes. He wasn't sure if the Phantoms made regular patrols of the area. That's what the two thugs he had run into before could have been doing. King recalled the four small boats they'd been standing next to, nothing but wooden hulls with motors attached. Maybe that was how the Phantoms transported their supply to Iquitos.

Maybe this river spiralled its way towards the city.

King stepped out of the rainforest briefly and peered downstream. Sure enough, he spotted the watercraft far in the distance, nothing but specks from here, bobbing on the flowing river's surface. They would provide a useful getaway instrument if he happened to successfully extract Burns and Norton.

Within five minutes he'd found a suitable shelter inside the rainforest. It was at the base of a small rocky outcrop jutting out from the side of a hill, situated close to the river. The natural formation created a dent in the hill, covered by plants and ferns and winding branches. A cove, hidden away from anyone in the area.

He nodded in approval and threw the duffel bag into the space created by the indentation. Now his gear was safe. The duffel had been a burden ever since he'd crashed into the trees earlier that morning. King looked up through the gaps in the canopy of trees, searching for the sun's location. It had reached its peak in the sky and was now in the long process of descending. He guessed it was around two in the afternoon. Plenty of time left to plan his attack.

He ducked into the shelter and unzipped the bag. Inside lay everything he needed for the rest of the operation. First, it was time to eat. He pulled out one of the ration packs and tore it open. The small package contained a power bar, a small tube of electrolytes and a tin of pre-cooked penne pasta. He wolfed the bar down, gulped the electrolytes then took his time with the pasta.

For the first time in the last twenty-four hours, he took a short break. He spent the period reflecting on where he was as he ate. He still had no backup, but he had a little more confidence now after laying eyes on the compound. It was larger than he thought it would be, and he had no doubt there was a means of communication somewhere within the main building. He would find it. He was sure of it. As for the hostages, that was a much more tentative situation.

Mabaya and the other Phantoms were fully prepared for a firefight. They were expecting him, and he was certain they would not hesitate to kill the two Americans without a second thought. King knew how hostage situations worked. Even if he managed to gain the upper hand in the battle, the thugs would still be able to kill the hostages with ease. And they would, if they were losing. A last resort to ensure King remained unsuccessful in his mission.

With a sick feeling in his stomach he tucked the remnants of his ration pack into the duffel and withdrew the MP5SD. For a submachine gun, the weapon was extremely precise. Exactly why King favoured it over other firearms. He'd used it for the past three years, and knew it inside and out. 30 round magazine. Just over seven pounds in weight. It could fire roughly 800 rounds a minute, which meant he could empty a clip in three seconds if he held down the trigger.

Useful for overwhelming violence.

His favourite kind of violence.

King slotted a spare magazine into his belt, brushed the ferns aside and rose out of the indent. It would do no good sitting on his rear and waiting for an opportune time to strike. He figured he would take some time to scout the surrounding area. Get used to the jungle. It would be disastrous if he got lost in the heat of combat.

He barely made it a step.

A stick snapping caught his attention, off to the side of his vision. He glanced over and saw three figures. Interspersed throughout the rainforest. All Phantoms. All armed.

They saw him.

CHAPTER 15

Two waves crashed through King at once.

The first was panic. His heart skipped a beat as he saw the three men make eye contact with him and begin to raise their weapons. They all appeared to be just as shocked to see him. Perhaps they hadn't been expecting someone to really be out in the rainforest. Perhaps they were rusty, having avoided combat for so long by setting up their facility in such a remote location.

The second thought that flooded his system was an urge to act. If he was to live, he had to rely on instincts and simply follow what felt natural. In this case, he raised the suppressed barrel of the MP5SD until it was level and pulled the trigger. The move was fast and fluid. Faster than the Phantoms. The kind of practiced reaction that came from spending half one's life in the heat of combat.

In just over two seconds he unloaded the magazine.

He swept the field of gunfire from left to right, drawing a horizontal line across the space in front of him.

When the gun clicked dry, thirty 9mm bullets were embedded in the torsos of the three men in front of him.

There had been no time for any of them to get a single shot off. King's reaction speed was unparalleled and he had used it here to devastating effect. Two of the men were thrown back by the force of the bullets, their chests scattered with holes. The third wasn't hit by as many. He remained standing. King got ready to dive for cover, but there was no need.

The man's gun — another Kalashnikov — fell from his hands. He looked down at his stomach, punctured by at least three rounds, then up at King. The blood had already drained from his face. He was pale.

On death's door.

He clutched feebly at his wounds, then fell back into a mass of branches. Already slipping from consciousness. He would be dead in seconds.

King was alive. His quick thinking had saved him from certain death. Now, though, there was a serious problem on his hands.

The MP5SD was equipped with a 5.7 inch barrel that decreased the noise of each bullet's report. It did this by reducing the pressure from each burst of gas that came from the ejection of a round. This was effective in situations where a slight reduction of noise would be beneficial. But the suppressor did not fully silence the submachine gun. No device could.

In the quiet of the rainforest, emptying a thirty-round magazine still sounded like a cacophony of unloaded ammunition.

Which — if King was back by the boats — would be inaudible to the compound.

But not from here. He was too close. He froze and listened for the sounds of chaos from the clearing.

Sure enough, there they were. Faint yelling. Commotion.

'Guns! Over there!'

'Did you hear that?!'

'Boys! Move out! He's here!'

'No, no, no, no,' King repeated under his breath.

The situation was disastrous. Three men were out of the equation but now every Phantom in the jungle had been made aware of his location.

They were coming.

King had to make sure of the impending pursuit before he took off. He stayed still for a moment longer, leaning against a tree, peering in the direction of the compound. Perhaps they didn't know exactly where the noises had come from.

Not ten seconds later he realised they knew.

Shapes began to materialise in the distance. The shapes formed rough silhouettes, which formed men. Lots of them. King counted at least ten, maybe even fifteen, growing closer *fast.* That was all he needed to see. A small army was heading for his position, armed to the teeth and more than ready to kill.

He turned and broke into a sprint for the river.

CHAPTER 16

Inside the compound, Mabaya crossed the main production room. This area was roughly the size of a warehouse, packed full of twisting steel pipes, shiny machines and industrial-size freezers. All carted in from the mainland, piece by piece. An operation that had taken years to set up, and had been running smoothly for the last eight months. Revenue had doubled over the last four. The Phantoms had risen from the laughing stock of the underworld to an unrivalled superpower in the narcotics industry. Half of Iquitos used their product. All from Mabaya's organisation skills and hard work.

There was no way he would let a single American fuck it all up.

He wiped the sweat off his brow and pushed open a door on the other side of the room. The hallway he stepped into was deserted. Most of his men had run off to kill the American pig. They would succeed. They outnumbered him ten to one.

Mabaya headed to the end of the hallway and kicked open a rickety wooden door, letting out some of the frustration of the morning. He stepped into a small dirty room with flaking white walls, stripped bare of any furniture. Previously, they'd used it as a storage area.

Now it held the hostages.

Mabaya looked down at them with contempt. They were separated from him by a wall of steel mesh, shoddily nailed into the walls halfway across the room. It divided the room into two halves, trapping his two prisoners on the other side. There were no windows in the room, no natural light. In here, there was no time. Nothing to base sleeping patterns on. Just a flickering halogen bulb screwed into a metal holster on the ceiling, dimly illuminating its contents.

And what abysmal contents they were.

The woman sat in one corner of the cell with her knees tucked up to her chest. Her eyes wide, her clothes torn. It had been a rough trip from the embassy to the compound. Many of his men had wanted her, but for now he had kept them at bay. He would save her for himself.

The boy in the corner looked shell-shocked. He'd never seen anything like this place. A sheltered little pussy, he was. He knew nothing of hardship, or violence, or fear. Mabaya would show him all three.

'Woman,' he said in English. She looked at him. Shivering. 'There is an American out there, in the jungle. Trying to save you. This makes me very angry. He has already killed a few of my men. Do you know about this?'

She shook her head. 'I have no idea what you're talking about.'

'I think you do,' Mabaya said, barely able to contain his rage. 'I think you've told the American where you are. No-one has found this place for years. Then when we take you two, someone stumbles across it. What are the chances of that?'

'I have nothing to do with this,' she said. He saw a tear roll down her cheek. The boy let out an audible sob.

Mabaya sneered. 'What the fuck are you crying about? You have nothing to cry about. Nothing's happened to you. But this American has made me very, very angry. When we kill him, I'll let all my men do whatever they want to you. You understand?'

A mixture of disgust and fear spread across her face. It was the reaction Mabaya was looking for. He turned to the boy, sitting in dishevelled clothing in the opposite corner. 'Some might want you too, bitch. I'll let them. I'll let them all.'

With that, he turned and left the room, slamming the door behind him. He despised foreigners.

The mental image of the horror on their faces would give him comfort for the rest of the day.

CHAPTER 17

King broke out of the trees into open space and took off along the banks of the river. He ran in a beeline, straight for the four boats in the distance. It was imperative that he got the fuck out of the area before he was shot to pieces.

It was paramount that he cover as much ground as possible before the men behind him made it out of the rainforest. There was nothing but wide open ground along the riverbank.

If his pursuers were half-competent, they would shoot him in the back without a moment's hesitation.

He had one clip of ammo on him. The rest of his gear was in the duffel bag, which would hopefully remain in the shelter he'd found. If that was located and removed, he was as good as dead.

Just as the boats came within close proximity, he heard shouting amongst the trees. He threw a glance back over his shoulder and baulked at the sight. Nine men had burst onto the riverbank, all carrying automatic rifles. A few of them were taking aim.

King wouldn't reach the nearest boat for at least three seconds. There was no cover to dive for. No action to take other than run for his life. He grit his teeth and pushed his legs as fast as they could possibly go, speeding across the uneven ground.

The first bullets whizzed past his head.

Usually King was prepared for any scenario. Even when rounds were flying, he had a talent for remaining calm.

Now, there was no staying calm.

He had never found himself in such a precarious scenario. If one bullet found its home, he would fall. The worst part was he would never see it coming.

Metal slugs hit the mud all around his feet. He heard the sound of their impact, ringing through his ears. Any moment he expected to have the lights go out. For a fleeting second, he wondered what death would feel like.

Then the boats were right there, and he was still alive. Using every ounce of energy he leapt into the footwell of the nearest vessel. He came down hard on the wooden floor. The pain of landing was almost a welcome feeling. At least he could still feel something.

The mercenaries were rusty with their aim, and it had saved his life. There wouldn't be much opportunity to practice firing at moving targets this far out in the rainforest. On top of that, ammunition was valuable out in these parts. Iquitos was a hundred miles away. He guessed the Phantoms did not churn through countless magazines of ammunition honing their aim.

As a result, they'd missed him. And now he would do everything in his power to ensure he seized the upper hand. He would never put himself in such a terrible situation again.

Bullets still flew above his head, but for now he was safe. The chassis of the boat blocked the Phantoms' line of sight. If King didn't get moving, they would catch up to him and unload their magazines into the boat. He was a sitting duck in his current position.

He crawled to the back of the boat and reached for the outboard motor. He wrapped one hand around the pull cord and gave it a heave. It spluttered, but did not start. Another hard tug and the motor roared to life. He slammed the throttle to its maximum output and pushed on the tiller so the small craft swung round in the water. A sudden jolt rattled him, throwing him across the floor. He realised the boat was still attached to its moorings, tied to the shore. It wouldn't budge.

He stayed flat on his stomach and reached up, searching for the attached rope. A bullet whisked by, so close that he could feel the displaced air. He wrapped his fingers around the thick nylon and wrenched it free. Then he re-engaged the throttle and the boat tore away from the shore.

He didn't dare raise his head. If he could see them, they could see him. Which meant a stray bullet could take his head off, no matter how terrible their aim was. They only needed to get lucky once.

He gauged his position in the river by lying flat on his back and studying the overhanging trees. The branches let him know if he was getting too close to either bank. Using this method he adjusted the tiller accordingly and guided the boat downstream at breakneck speed.

The river was shallow, and as a result the hull crushed against rocks at high velocity. King felt the reverberations through his body after each impact. Behind him he heard the revving of engines and realised that the Phantoms had spread out amongst the three remaining boats.

They were giving chase.

Not ideal.

King took a moment to gather his thoughts, then switched to a crouch. The men would be preoccupied with steering their boats. They wouldn't have him in their sights. Not yet.

Even if they were waiting for him to show himself, they wouldn't come close to landing a shot. The river flowed fast, making it impossible to hold a weapon steady. The only way he would be hit was through blind luck. Which was possible, but worth taking a risk to check their position.

The three boats were at different stages of giving pursuit. One had surged ahead from the others, gaining rapidly on King. Four men perched in its small frame. The others were in the process of leaving shore. One boat contained three men and the other housed a pair.

Nine Phantoms in total.

The men in the lead boat saw him. One steered the outboard motor while the other three scooped up their weapons. King saw three barrels swing in his direction and dove back underneath the frame, just as a wave of bullets lit up the space over his head. He'd been wrong about the accuracy of the hostiles. They were much closer than he originally assumed.

The shooting did not stop. King flattened himself against the floor and listened to all three men unload their magazines at his boat. A few bullets punctured the flimsy wooden hull, but none struck him. Finally, after what felt like an eternity, the barrage ceased.

An idea came to him.

He reached up and eased off the throttle, then swung the tiller round so that the bow aimed toward the opposite bank. The boat slowed and began to drift. King stayed out of sight of the pursuing Phantoms. Within a few seconds, he felt the craft run into a cluster of low-hanging branches on the other side of the river and grind to a halt, firmly entangled in the scrub.

He killed the motor.

Silence.

Now he could hear the whining of the other three boats. He managed to roughly gauge their position from what was audible. The first boat was fast approaching. His plan was working.

They thought he was dead.

To them, it appeared he had been riddled with bullets and lost control of the boat, and his corpse now lay in the bottom of the damaged wreck.

They were coming to check.

That would be their downfall.

Silently, King reloaded the MP5SD. He ejected the empty magazine and slotted in the fresh 30-round clip attached to his belt. It was all the ammunition he had left. Hopefully, it was all he would need.

He waited, lying prone, until it felt like the other boat was right on top of him. He heard the four men shuffle around, creaking wood. The man driving let off the throttle. The engine grew quieter.

Now.

King burst off the floor of his boat and unloaded all thirty rounds into their vessel before any of them had the slightest chance to react.

CHAPTER 18

Their boat turned to a bloodbath.

The entirety of his magazine poured across the vessels. It had a devastating effect on the occupants. All four men jerked like marionettes on strings. All four lost their lives in a single moment. All four careered out of the boat, splashing one by one into the murky water.

King fired until his gun clicked empty. He knew if he successfully eliminated all four of them, there would be spare weapons in their boat that he could ravage. It was worth overcompensating by unloading his whole magazine to ensure he was the only one in the vicinity left breathing. It would be disastrous to leave one man alive and risk getting shot back.

The enemy boat had been drifting toward his. In an instant it was empty. It continued on its path, carried by momentum and the current of the river. King watched it enter the same branches his had. Then its bow slammed into the side of his boat.

At that exact moment, he leapt across. He landed on a smear of blood left over from the deaths of its four occupants. The puddle was slick and unstable. He slid on the wet patch and crashed to the floor, coming down hard. It didn't matter. He was in. There were six men left to take care of, and then Mabaya's forces would be severely incapacitated.

'Light work,' he muttered, trying to convince himself that what lay ahead would be an easy task.

This boat was slightly different, he noted. Its frame rose a little higher on all sides, giving him enough room to crouch and remain out of sight of the other two boats. Two guns had been discarded on the floor. The other two had stayed with their owners as all four men fell overboard, heading straight for a watery grave.

King checked the position of the four bodies around the boat. The corpses were already out of sight. They'd sunk fast. Even a couple of feet below the surface, the river was murky enough to make them disappear. King breathed a sigh of relief that they had died instantly. Drowning was a method of death that he wished on no man, not even those trying to kill him. He believed that — save a few exceptions — everyone deserved a quick death.

The two boats behind him had finally left shore. They roared toward him. The vessel on the left held the pair of Phantoms, while the other held three. King used the short time he had in which there was significant distance between them to swing the tiller of his new boat around and gun the engine in their direction. The bow arced through the water until it aimed for a collision course with the boat on the left, then held still. A game of chicken on the rough waters of the river.

As soon as King guided the boat on course, he dropped. The gunfire from the Phantoms was inevitable. And the closer they got, the higher their chance of landing a shot. It would only take one to eliminate him from the fight.

The two rifles on the floor beside him were both Kalashnikovs. It seemed the Phantoms had ordered a bulk lot of the same brand. Probably off the black market. Whatever the case, one was another AK-74 and the second was a newer, cleaner AK-105. Very similar weapons. They both used the same caliber of ammunition. It would not matter which he selected. What did matter was which one had any bullets left in the magazine. There was no time to check. He simply had to guess.

He heard the enemy boat buzzing closer. It wouldn't be long before they collided, unless someone swerved out of the way. And King sure as hell wasn't going to. He couldn't even see what lay ahead. A few bullets thunked into the bow. The Phantoms were firing warning shots. Attempting to scare him into changing course.

He didn't budge.

Still crouching low, he snatched up the AK-105, pointed its barrel towards the sky and held the trigger.

Bang, bang, bang.

Three bullets left in the magazine, all loud and unsuppressed and ejecting from the barrel in rapid succession.

He knew it would send them ducking for cover.

Now, the hard part. Would they swerve to the left or the right? He had one attempt at his next move. If the timing was a fraction of a second wrong, he'd die. If his reflexes were not sharp enough, he'd die.

If anything at all did not go according to plan, he'd die.

He guessed the Phantom driving the boat was more than likely right handed, and as such his instincts would cause him to involuntarily swing to the right in order to avoid a collision. He tensed the muscles in his legs and took a deep inhalation. Ready to jump.

Just as the whining of the enemy boat's engine reached a crescendo, King sprung off the floor of his, took a single step and launched off the side of the boat.

He'd guessed correctly.

The enemy boat was in the process of passing by. Exactly where he'd decided to jump. Both members of the boat had their heads down, still reeling from the sudden burst of gunfire that had come from King's craft. They weren't expecting what came next in the slightest.

King landed double-footed, effectively leap-frogging between the two boats. He never stopped moving. Using his forward momentum he charged at the nearest hostile. The man held an automatic rifle, but he wouldn't have time to use it. King dropped his shoulder low. Pushed off the floor with all the power in his glutes. Thundered his bulk into the man's chest.

Two hundred pounds of sprinting muscle knocked the mercenary senseless. The gun flew from his hands and the impact took him off his feet. Straight off the edge of the boat.

King didn't even pause to watch him hit the water. He heard the splash as he turned to face the second man, registering that the first was momentarily out of the equation. The driver wasn't armed. Both his hands still rested on the tiller. His Kalashnikov lay at his feet. It would be no use to him there.

King wound up and threw a well-practiced uppercut with his right hand. He planted his feet before the swing, lending it the power of his legs. Momentum transitioned from his feet to his thighs to his torso, shooting through his shoulder as he arced around. The driver didn't stand a chance. King's knuckles crashed against the soft tissue under his chin. His brain rattled hard in his skull, which was the only thing necessary to strip away his consciousness. His legs gave out and he collapsed to the floor, out for at least the next thirty seconds.

This wasn't the movies. He would soon come to his senses. No-one stayed down for more than a minute. But the concussion would disorientate him enough to put him out of the equation for the foreseeable future.

King's plan had worked flawlessly so far. There was just one boat left, still a fair distance away. Three hostiles were perched within.

He dropped his guard for a single second.

That was all it took.

One of the thugs in the final boat fired a round from his automatic weapon, probably a Kalashnikov. A single round shot across the space of the river before King had time to blink and buried itself deep in his left wrist. A white hot burst of pain flooded his senses and he instinctively dove to the floor of the boat.

Blood began to pour from the wound.

CHAPTER 19

King was prepared for injuries, but it didn't change the pain associated with such a grievous wound. The bullet had embedded itself deep in his skin. It was a grisly sight, already dripping crimson.

He recognised the pain associated with a 5.45x39mm round. They were often labelled "poison bullets" from those hit by them. They fragmented and tumbled upon impact, causing massive damage to tissue. King wasn't sure of the severity, but he needed a temporary fix for the problem before the final boat caught up to him and filled him with lead.

He withdrew two items from a small pouch on the side of his belt. Thankfully, both were untouched by the chaos of the morning. One was a sterilised set of tiny pliers, and the other was a minuscule canister of superglue. The two things King had found most effective for quickly stopping blood flow on the battlefield. He'd experienced his fair share of combat wounds in the past. He stayed level-headed as he got to work.

Being the most effective method did not make it the least painful. In fact, King found it quite the contrary. He dug the pliers into the wound, crushing his teeth together in an attempt to combat his screaming nerve endings. Each tooth of the pliers locked onto either side of the bullet and he ripped it free. He let out a roar as fire flooded his brain. The pain began to verge on the edge of unbearable. Any worse, and he would pass out from the agony.

The hole in his wrist needed patching up, fast. Thankfully King had the other item. He unscrewed the small lid to the superglue and upended the container into the wound. It came out as a clear liquid and instantly began to set. It stung like all hell. King clenched his fists until his knuckles turned white. A feeble attempt to ride out the pain.

He heard the last boat closing in.

He snatched up the unconscious driver's AK-74 and fired a blind volley of shots over the edge of the frame, aiming in their general direction. A simultaneous burst of fire greeted him back, splintering the wooden hull of his boat. One round punctured the flimsy frame and whisked past his face, close enough that he could feel the displaced air against his forehead.

He panicked. The boat was a death trap. These men had watched their comrades get shot to pieces. They were ready for any assault King threw at them. They had their aim locked on. There was no way he could win this one.

King managed to stay alive in these types of situations partially because of his combat skills, but mostly because he could recognise when it was time to retreat. By the time he rose out of cover and managed to achieve any sort of decent aim on the enemy boat, they would riddle his body with bullets.

Time to go.

King sucked as much air into his lungs as possible and held the breath for five long seconds. Then he exhaled slowly, forcing the precarious situation he was in from his mind, doing everything in his power to calm down. He would need it for what lay ahead. He ignored the sound of the final boat droning steadily toward him. It would do no good to worry about that. Reducing his heartbeat was the only thing on his mind. He let the adrenalin of combat flow out of his system.

He took a final inhale, deep and full, letting it resonate throughout his body. Then wrapped one hand around the frame. Got his legs underneath him. Rolled over the side. Dropped silently into the murky river.

They would have seen him enter the water, but he would be impossible to locate. The river was filthy, and as King plunged into it his vision turned to black. Nothing was visible under its surface.

To guarantee he wasn't spotted he swam a few feet straight down. Now they would be clueless as to his location. Underneath the water, there was no sound. It was eerily quiet in contrast to the constant gunshots and the screaming of outboard motors.

King set off, his pace measured. A year of training with the Navy SEALs at the very beginning of his military career had left him with the ability to hold his breath for up to four minutes. He hadn't spent long with the SEALs. Even as a novice in terms of military experience his potential had quickly been realised and he had shot through the ranks, eventually contracted to a division that the public wasn't aware existed. But the training stuck with him.

All his training stuck with him.

He tried to forget that three hostiles were somewhere above his head, their guns most likely trained toward the water. It would only take one fluke shot to kill him. He forced the thought from his mind and focused on a steady breaststroke, aiming for the opposite riverbank. His current priority was making it ashore without any of the three remaining Phantoms realising.

Then a bullet sliced through the water less than a foot beside him.

His first thought was instant panic, but he didn't allow himself to physically react. It took every ounce of restraint in his body to stay calm. Any sudden movements would cause stirring at the water's surface. He had to float still and pray that it had been nothing but a stray shot.

There were no further shots. He had no way of knowing where the three Phantoms were above him. Everything stayed shrouded in darkness. He couldn't see up or down or left or right. Nothing to do but continue swimming.

A tightness began to snake its way into his chest. He felt the restriction of air starting to take effect. He'd only been under for perhaps a minute and a half, but the conditions were less than perfect. When he'd held his breath for four minutes in the SEAL training facilities, it had been in big pools of crystal clear water. No-one shooting at him, looking to end his life. No unstable conditions. Just him and the water and intense concentration.

This warzone was vastly different to the training pool.

Mapping his course in his head using nothing but his memory, he powered on. Kicking steadily, hands slicing through the murky water ahead. Slow, controlled movements. The restriction of air started to bother him. Severely. He tried not to let it faze him. With his throat burning and chest expanding he continued to swim forward, always forward, never stopping, never slowing.

The opposite riverbank had to be here somewhere. It felt like he had crossed the length of the river a thousand times. Still, nothing but darkness and muddy water ahead. He couldn't resurface. They'd see him. They'd pick him off with ease. He had to fight against his lungs, now screaming for air.

Keep going.

He reached out blindly, feeling, searching, fingers reaching for anything that could be the riverbank.

Just as black spots appeared in the centre of his vision his hands plunged into mud. He took a second to feel around. He had come to a steady slope that reached diagonally toward the surface. The shore.

With his wrist and his lungs both in equal amounts of pain, he fumbled up the underwater hill until the surface was right there above his head. It was paramount that he avoided taking a loud gasp of air when he broke out. The enemy boat's engine and the noise of the flowing river would more than likely drown out any sound he made, but one could never be too cautious.

He exited the water and crawled up the muddy banks, inhaling quietly. Water dripped off his khakis. He turned to see the three-man boat patrolling the opposite side of the river, one man steering and the other two peering down, trying to spot any sign of movement underneath the surface. The other three boats drifted slowly along the river, carried by the current, all empty except for the one Phantom coming out of unconsciousness. If King counted correctly, there were five men at the bottom of the river.

And three left to take care of.

Unarmed and gasping for breath, it would be hard to achieve anything in his present state. He needed the duffel bag.

Was there time to retrieve it?

The three Phantoms still on the hunt had yet to spot him. They weren't looking in his direction. None of them had expected him to cover the distance he had, and as such they were searching in entirely the wrong location. He still had time to return to his shelter.

He got to his feet and crept up the riverbank, heading for the rainforest. Once inside, they would never find him. He would disappear. But it was urgent that he return to finish them off, or they would head back to Mabaya and raise the alarm.

Then the two remaining hostages would be slaughtered.

King passed between two trees and entered the jungle.

CHAPTER 20

The shelter was exactly how he'd left it, small and hidden and scattered with the litter of his mid-afternoon meal. His duffel lay open. He hadn't had time to close it before the three-man search party had crept up on him and everything had gone to shit.

The natural sounds of the rainforest had returned in all their subtle details. Calls and shrieks of wildlife sounded all around him, some close, some far in the distance. The jungle had returned to its status quo as the conflict raged elsewhere.

King withdrew the FN-SCAR-L rifle from the bag. The L stood for light. There was a heavy model too, complete with higher-caliber ammunition, but that model didn't suit close quarters combat in the rainforest. He'd requested something agile and reliable. Nothing better than the SCAR. Designed for SOCOM, there was no reason for him to use anything else. They'd offered him brand new, state-of-the-art gear reserved for the special forces. He'd declined. The SCAR had everything he wanted. It was a chunky beast of an assault rifle, currently used by more than twenty countries. He didn't have time for expensive accessories.

He slung the strap connecting the SCAR's magazine to its stock over his shoulder, snatched a few more supplies, zipped up the duffel and set off for the river.

It was a strange experience being in such a desolate part of the planet. The only human activity within a hundred miles was a gang of drug dealers looking to end his life. Other than that, he was alone in a dense, inhospitable region that spanned entire countries. He felt awe every time he considered the size of the Amazon Rainforest, so much of it unexplored. It was likely that if he chose a random direction and set off, he would find himself in a patch of jungle never touched by humans.

As he strode for the last location he'd seen the boats, he took a look at the wound on his wrist. Adrenalin had numbed the injury, but for now the bleeding had ceased. The superglue had dried, leaving a yellow layer caked over the wound. He would let a doctor patch it up properly when he was back in safe hands.

Sure enough, the enemy boat still patrolled the waters as he reached the section of rainforest nearest the docking poles. King dropped to one knee and raised the SCAR, resting the stock against his shoulder. The stock gave him a platform to steady his aim, which was accurate enough regardless. He exhaled and held still. He did not move a muscle. He aligned the SCAR's optics with the boat on the other side of the river.

The driver would be the easiest target. He stood fully upright while the other two men squatted low, peering off each edge of the boat into the flowing river water. Still trying to locate King in the river, when in actuality he was a hundred feet away, lining up to put a bullet into each of their skulls.

King squeezed off a volley. The report in his ear was deafening, but there was no ear protection out here in the field. He would just have to put up with it. Four 45mm rounds spat out of the barrel and covered the space between them in less than a tenth of a second. Three hit the driver. The fourth shot away into the rainforest on the other side. Not that King saw any of that. He simply tapped the trigger and watched through the sights as the driver jerked off his feet, crumpling to the floor of the boat and disappearing from sight.

Either dead, or very close to.

The other two promptly jumped a foot each, startled by the sudden turn of events. King saw them both dive for cover. He gave them credit. They'd reacted with animalistic fervour. Survival mode had kicked in. He hadn't had time to fire at them.

Ears ringing, he watched them reach for the tiller and swing the boat around so the bow was facing his side of the shore.

Then they accelerated. Just as he had done. A smart move. He had nothing to shoot at.

For a moment, he hesitated. He'd picked up an extra magazine for the SCAR before he returned. But it would do no good to waste all the rounds in his current one firing at the boat, hoping to hit a target through the wooden hull with a stroke of blind luck. The likely result would be that he ran out of ammunition just as the boat ploughed onto the shore. Which would be disadvantageous, to say the least.

The pair had made a smart move, he had to admit. King had expected panic, retreat, terror. The sort of uncoordinated reactions that came with seeing a close ally picked off from a distance. But they'd quickly assessed where the threat had come from and subsequently charged toward it.

Exactly what King would have done.

Perhaps these two would put up a different fight to the rest of them. So far the mercenaries' actions had been predictable. Tough to deal with, but predictable. The type of behaviour King had seen a million times before. Which was what had allowed him to stay alive.

So far.

He decided to retreat deep into cover and wait for the boat to crash into the riverbank. When the pair rose above the frame, he would be ready. He would shoot them dead. Then he would move on.

Water frothed at the bow of the boat as it speared horizontally across the river toward his position. For a man steering blind, whoever had control of the tiller was incredibly precise. It would run aground directly in front of King. He began to doubt himself. Maybe they knew something he didn't. He'd expected a quick and painless execution of the three men, from far away. Now the two left alive were threatening to turn the fight into a close-quarters gunfight. Something which he always strived to avoid unless absolutely necessary.

The bow slammed into the mud, tossing up a wave of it. King kept his eye planted against his sights. Searching for a fraction of movement. Anything to shoot at. He would open fire as soon as he saw either of the two men. He hoped his reflexes were faster than theirs.

Nothing happened. The boat slid to a halt and silence lapsed over the river. The engine died as the propellor clogged with mud. King didn't hear a peep from inside its frame.

What's happening? he thought. Unsure how to react.

A pair of hands darted into view. Clutching a Kalashnikov rifle. This one an AK-105. King caught a glimpse of the gun and abandoned his SCAR. It wasn't worth risking his life to shoot his enemy in the hand. He just got below a fallen log before a wild spray from the rifle ripped through the vegetation all around him.

Even after years of service, King hated getting shot at, no matter how safe he considered his cover to be. It came with the unpleasant knowledge that it would only take a single stray round to ricochet off something hard and catapult into his vital organs, and that would be that. He rode out the feeling of terror until the gunfire ceased.

Back to silence. Now, his position was even worse. They could be aiming at the last place they'd seen him. Just waiting for him to stick his head out into the open so they could blast it apart.

He could either act now, or never act at all.

He gripped the SCAR tight and shot out from behind the fallen log. The riverbank came into view. An empty boat. Both men were in the process of vaulting out of it. Both wielding assault rifles. They'd assumed King would stay in cover, fearing more shots. They'd decided to take advantage of the tables turning and get out of their vessel.

They'd assumed wrong.

King reacted in a split second. He swung his aim round to the man on the left, who was mid-leap. Still airborne. He held the trigger and lit him up with at least five or six bullets. They exited the gun too fast for him to count. Whatever the case, the man died. Fast.

King released the trigger and turned to fire a similar volley at the man on the right.

Then he realised he'd misjudged it.

Which proved disastrous.

The last Phantom left alive on the river had already landed on shore by the time King took aim. He already had his Kalashnikov up, barrel locked on.

He pulled his own trigger and shot King in the chest.

CHAPTER 21

Inside the compound, Mabaya's radio squawked to life. A sharp burst of static followed by a couple of sentences, short and sharp. He recognised the voice. Deep and confident. It was Armando.

'Boss, I hit the American. He's down.'

Mabaya snatched the satellite phone off his belt and thumbed a button on its side.

'Is he dead?'

'He's wounded. But I'm in control. Want me to bring him in?'

'Yes. Let's hang him up and cut him until he's dry. Slowly. Fucking pig. How many of you are there?'

A short pause. Mabaya didn't like the sound of that. Then came the reply. 'None.'

He wasn't sure he'd heard correctly. Perhaps Armando had said *nine*. There was no inconceivable way that a single man had slaughtered more than half his men.

'What did you say?'

'I said none. He killed them all. I…'

Mabaya heard something that sounded very much like a sob. He didn't blame the man. Out here in the uninhabited rainforest, the Phantoms were the only humans for miles in any direction. Friendships formed quickly. And this fucker had stripped them all away.

'If you want to kill him now, Armando, do it. I don't care.'

'Thanks, boss. See you soon.'

Static, then silence.

A slight grin spread across Mabaya's face as he imagined what Armando would do to the American. It would be long and drawn-out and painful, fuelled by the deaths of his friends. That thought quickly wiped the smile away. As dawn broke earlier that morning, twenty-two Phantoms had occupied the facility. The maximum amount of men they kept in this place at one time. Now fourteen were dead. The two who he'd sent to tend to the boats earlier that morning had never returned, so he counted them out. After he'd killed the bald hostage he'd sent out a search party of three men to look for the American. Next came a cacophony of gunfire, meaning they'd made contact. Also meaning they were probably dead. So he'd sent out the bulk of his forces. Nine men.

There was one left alive.

The day's events would leave a sizeable hole in his operation. Perhaps it would be compromised forever. Mabaya didn't know how many more Americans would come, and what this one had achieved was already devastating. He did not know where he would go from here.

Anger swelled within him. He rose off the rickety chair he had been perched on and lashed out, kicking it across the room.

Thankfully, there were two hostages in the back room he could happily take out his anger on.

He turned and walked down the hallway to their cell.

CHAPTER 22

The bullet hit King like every other battlefield wound he'd sustained did.

So fast he didn't see it coming.

It was a strange feeling. One moment he had his aim locked on, ready to kill the final Phantom on the river. The next he felt a searing pain near his shoulder and before he knew it the SCAR had dropped from his hands. He lost his footing and fell into the undergrowth. It probably saved his life. As he collapsed, a cluster of AK-105 rounds flew over his head. They would have killed him instantly had he still been standing upright.

In the heat of battle, King's first instinct was always to act. No matter how dire the situation. Forward momentum was critical to survival. So despite the wound he urged himself to get to his feet, before even calculating the severity of the injury.

When his body didn't respond, he knew it was bad.

The shock of getting hit shut down his system. The pain had yet to come. But it would. Even though it wasn't instantaneous, it would surface shortly. After the shell-shock wore off.

The SCAR had fallen into a cluster of plants, just out of reach. King made a move for it, urging his muscles to act, but before he could get hold of it the man who had shot him stepped over a log and planted a boot into his chest. Pinning him into place.

King took a look at the man who would probably end his life. He'd shaved his hair on the sides and let the top grow long and straggly. It looked like it hadn't been washed in months. He had beady eyes, a weather-beaten face lined with contours and a thick scar running down his left cheek. The expression on his face was one of fury. He aimed the barrel of his weapon right between King's eyes. King knew any wrong move on his part would be met with a bullet in the brain.

'I call boss,' he said in stunted English. 'Then I kill you.'

'Sounds good,' King said.

The man put more pressure on King's chest, causing him to cough violently. 'Think you're funny, huh, American?'

King didn't reply. He could already feel blood begin to seep from the wound in his shoulder. It flowed down his arm, hot and wet.

The man withdrew a thick satellite phone from his back pocket and thumbed a few buttons. King felt a slight stab of hope. If he could make it out of this situation somehow, someway, then he would be able to contact reinforcements.

The man began to converse with someone on the other end of the line, speaking fluent Spanish. He spoke too fast for King to decipher each word but he managed to translate a few in his head.

Specifically, '*Kill him now, Armando,*' from the other end.

The man named Armando smiled as he hung up. There would be adrenalin flowing through him as he prepared to kill. King knew exactly what that felt like.

He also knew it made you careless.

Armando took the pressure off King's chest as he hung up, his mind elsewhere. It gave just enough room for King to shift his weight and slide his good hand behind his back. Reaching for the back of his belt. Fingers searching desperately for the object he'd placed there not ten minutes earlier. The object that had been pinned under his bulk the entire time.

With a flood of relief, he found it.

The spare Glock 19.

King ripped it free and swung his arm out, barrel pointed at Armando's forehead. The mercenary had made a fatal mistake. He'd let his aim wander. He'd thought King was defenceless. The AK-105 now wavered in his hand, aimed just a few inches past King's head.

A careless and stupid mistake. One that would cost him dearly.

King shot him in the face without a shadow of remorse.

Armando fell back, relieving King of his weight. He crashed against the log he'd stepped over and came to rest in a sitting position. Stone dead. King saw blood pool from his forehead, thick and viscous. The same colour as the liquid currently leaking from his shoulder.

He rolled over and clambered to his knees. Renewed with a newfound determination. The mission was still salvageable. There was still hope, no matter how slim. The agony in his shoulder made his nerve endings scream, threatened to break him. He wouldn't let it.

The bullet in his shoulder had ripped through the khaki material of his shirt, leaving a jagged gash. He dug his fingers into the gap and tore off the sleeve, revealing a muscular arm devoid of fat. His shoulder was already covered in blood. King tied the strip of material tight around his shoulder, looping it under his armpit and pulling it just tight enough to avoid cutting off circulation. It was a temporary fix to a serious problem, but it would do for now. The crude bandaging would ensure he didn't bleed out from his wounds in the near future. He just needed long enough to finish his job. Besides, backup would be here soon.

He reached for the satellite phone Armando had dropped into the undergrowth. Just as he wrapped his fingers around the device, it crackled to life.

'Armando, wait…' the voice said in Spanish. 'I want the American alive. Bring him here.'

King froze. Armando wouldn't be replying anytime soon. King couldn't speak Spanish well enough to pass off as the mercenary. He would simply have to ignore the request and wait to see what happened.

Nothing further came from the phone. King rose to his feet, tentative. He winced as the bullet in his shoulder sent stabs of fire through his upper chest. It would be a long recovery before he was back to full health. And he was still far from done.

'Armando,' the voice said again. This time urgent. Insistent. Demanding a response.

King said nothing. A button on the side of the phone would enable him to reply, but he did not use it. He couldn't.

Now the voice switched to English. A bad sign. 'If there is no reply in one minute, I will kill the hostages. You hear that, American? One minute. Then they are dead.'

Panic washed over King. He swore and tucked the satellite phone into one pocket of his khakis. There was no time to use it. There was no time to do anything now except run. He scooped up the SCAR, ignoring the pain from his wrist and shoulder. It did not concern him anymore. Two innocent people would die if he didn't make it to the compound as fast as humanly possible.

Every step sent waves of pain and nausea across his shoulder, his chest, his arm, his wrist. He forced all of them aside. He pictured Burns and Norton, curled up somewhere inside the facility, fearing for their lives. It was all he needed. He burst out onto the riverbank and sprinted like a madman in the direction of the compound.

Hoping he wasn't too late.

CHAPTER 23

By the time he made it to the area of rainforest where he'd last seen the compound, no more than two or three minutes had elapsed. His breath rasped and his chest burned and his legs were weak but he barely even noticed. His right arm ached from wielding the bulk of the SCAR, but he had no other option than to use it one-handed. His left arm was all but useless.

Grunting in agony, he dropped to the forest floor a safe distance away from the facility. Then came the crawl. It mirrored his last approach not an hour earlier, but this time he bore the full effects of combat. Each movement felt twice as difficult. His energy ran low. But people needed him, as they always did, so he would persevere. He knew nothing else.

The moment he laid eyes on the clearing in front of the facility he knew instantly that his efforts had been futile. The two hostages stood side-by-side, facing out into the jungle. Both quaking. Both pale. Behind them, Mabaya had a bulky pistol in each hand. His arms were spread wide, in a V-shape. He pointed a barrel at each of the Americans' heads.

Burns and Norton.

It was the first time King had seen either of them.

Both looked nothing like the neat, orderly passport photos he had been shown in the hangar the night before. Burns' secretarial uniform was torn to shreds, a result of the tough journey through the rainforest or perhaps something worse. Her hair hung wild and frizzy on either side, the ponytail gone. Nevertheless she stood tall, shoulders straight. Defiant even in such a terrible position. King admired her nerve.

Norton had broken mentally. Even from a distance away, that much was apparent. He trembled uncontrollably, clothes also torn, hair matted to his forehead, blood caked on his cheeks. His youth meant inexperience, and inexperience meant he had been wholly unprepared for the brutality of a Peruvian drug gang. King wondered the consequences for his mental health even if he made it out of the jungle alive.

Right then and there, King vowed he would do everything in his power to make sure the two of them lived. Although with each passing second, that seemed to be a less likely scenario.

'American!' Mabaya roared. 'I see you moving out there! Stand up right now. No gun. If you don't, I'll kill them both. And then we'll kill you anyway.'

King knew the chances of a successful extraction had all but disappeared. His situation was beyond dire. There were few options left. In his haste, he had failed to call for backup. No-one was coming for him. His injuries were significant, his resources were exhausted and he had nothing to do but surrender. If he gave it any more thought, innocents would die. They would probably die anyway, but he couldn't stand to sit here and watch them. He would either join them in death, or they would somehow make it out alive.

He dropped the SCAR rifle and stood up.

Burns let out an audible gasp. King knew what the sound meant. It meant the fraction of hope she had been holding onto was now gone, taken away by the surrender of the man she believed would rescue her. It was tough to watch the light drain from her eyes. King watched her accept her own death. It shook him to his core.

Norton was beyond caring. It seemed he had accepted his own death hours ago, perhaps even the day before when he had been taken from the embassy. He didn't move a muscle as King rose out of the ferns into view. Just stared vacantly into the distance. Terrified. Shaking.

'Ah!' Mabaya roared as King appeared. 'There we are! The man who killed half my fucking men!'

'That's me,' King said. He tried to keep a brave face but it was tough. Especially when, for the first time in his life, he was certain he would die. Usually he had a way out. A backup plan, even in the most dire situations.

Not this time.

If Mabaya wanted, he could kill all three of them right there and then without a second thought. But he didn't. Either pride, or curiosity, or something else got the better of him. He wanted to see King up close. The American who'd decimated his forces single-handedly.

'Come here,' he said, his voice full of hate. 'Now!'

King took a step toward the clearing.

'Hands in the fucking air! And take that gun out of your belt.'

King couldn't comprehend how Mabaya had even seen the Glock resting in its holster against his rear. Nevertheless, his final sliver of hope faded away. He reached back, withdrew the gun and threw it into the undergrowth. There was no use trying to fire a lucky shot at Mabaya. Even if he hit him, both pistols would go off and Burns and Norton would die.

King continued walking toward the clearing, making sure to take his time. His wounds hurt like all hell, especially the superglued bullet hole in his wrist. The shoddy patch-up job would have severe consequences if he didn't get medical treatment in the next couple of days. Heading for Mabaya, he wasn't sure he would be alive to see the next morning.

He stepped out onto the grassy clearing floor. Mabaya didn't falter. He kept his guns trained firmly on the two hostages. Up close, King recognised the make of the weapons. They were both FN Browning High Power Mk. III's. Popular with law enforcement. Probably purchased on the black market. It didn't matter what make they were, though. They were guns. They would send a bullet tumbling through both hostages' skulls, killing them instantly.

'Who the fuck are you?' Mabaya said.

'Just trying to get my friends back,' King said. 'Simple as that.'

'Who sent you?'

'Nobody.'

'I know someone sent you. From America.'

'You're right. Someone did. But you'll have never heard of them. They're classified.'

'You killed all my men.'

'I did. Thirteen of them.'

Mabaya hesitated. 'I sent out fourteen.'

'One's still alive, out on one of the boats. Recovering from a concussion.'

'How did you do this?'

'A lot of training.'

'They were my friends.'

King gestured to Burns and Norton. 'These are mine. The American you killed was my friend.'

His expression hardened. 'Good. American pigs. You will all die. Motherfuckers. You stay the fuck out of our business.'

'You shot up our embassy. We didn't provoke you.'

'Police were taking our location to you. You would have killed us all.'

'No, we wouldn't have.'

Mabaya gnashed his teeth together, his face all rage and fury. King knew there was no reasoning with him. He hated Americans with a passion. Nothing would change that.

'Now!' he barked.

King didn't even hear the movement behind him until it was too late. He heard the rustle of leaves from the forest floor and then a slight sensation of displaced air behind his neck, like something swinging through the air. A fist crashed into the top of his spine. A blow wound up from a sizeable distance away. Full of power, strength, primal anger. His legs buckled from the force of the punch and he dropped to his knees. He careered forward onto the clearing floor. Dazed. Disoriented.

He just managed to turn his head in time to see the second punch coming. Too fast to dodge. Too powerful to absorb. The Phantom's knuckles crashed against his jaw with perfect placement. He felt a sharp explosion of nerve endings across the side of his face. Then his vision went black. His senses faded.

Darkness.

CHAPTER 24

Everyone feels the same thing when they resurface from unconsciousness.

A sense of utter confusion.

It felt like no time had passed at all. King's head swam as he came to, and he found himself wondering where the hell he was and how on earth he had managed to get there. He was lying on the floor of a small concrete room. Whitewashed walls. He blinked hard. Two people watched him. A youthful guy and an older woman. He studied their faces. They wore expressions of shock and fear and apprehension. Not your standard emotions.

Where was he?

Bits and pieces began to come back. Some kind of a foreign environment. A rainforest. That's where he'd been. He hadn't felt safe either. Tension and unease knotted his gut.

'Are you okay?' the woman said.

King raised a hand to his temple and rubbed it. His eyes throbbed from the artificial light overhead.

'Yeah,' he said. 'I'll be fine. I've been concussed before.'

The murky haze grew clearer. He remembered where he was, and why he was there.

'You're Burns?' he said.

The woman nodded. 'And you're the man everyone's been looking for.'

King turned to the boy. 'Norton?'

He nodded too. A timid gesture, full of fear.

'We're fucked, aren't we?' Norton said. 'You were our last hope. We're going to die in here. Oh my god…'

The room was small and square and dirty. King turned and noticed they were caged in. Thick steel mesh stretched from wall to wall in the centre of the room, blocking their path to the door on the other side. The space felt cramped, entirely devoid of windows or any external light.

'I've been in worse situations,' King said, still looking around, too busy to make eye contact. 'We may have a shot.'

'Are you crazy?' Burns said. 'One of them is going to walk through that door any second and either torture us or kill us.'

'He'll probably just shoot us, if that's any consolation,' King said. 'I think he knows if he comes in here and tries anything I'll put up a fight. He saw what I did to his men.'

'What did you do to his men?' Burns said. 'For the last few hours this place has been pandemonium. Shouting, screaming. I heard so many gunshots in the distance…'

'I killed about half his forces, but evidently that wasn't enough.'

He saw Norton's eyes widen. Beads of sweat ran down his forehead.

'You okay, kid?'

The boy shook his head. 'I … I don't know if you two are used to this kind of situation, or whatever, but I can't handle this. I'm going to fucking die in here. Do you get it? We're going to die…'

He began to repeat the same train of thought over and over again. Muttering, most of it inaudible, all of it concerning death.

King reached out and grabbed him by the shoulders. 'Look, this is tough. You've never been scared for your life before. And by that I mean genuinely terrified. I have. It's not a good feeling but you can't let it consume you. Stay strong. I'm gonna try and get us out of here but you can't have a fucking mental breakdown while I'm trying.'

'You're a soldier?' Norton asked, his voice shaking.

'Kind of.'

'How do you do this? How do you just sit there and tell me everything's going to be fine when we're sitting in a room waiting to be raped or killed.'

'Like I said, I've been in worse situations. Look at me. I'm still here.'

'Why do you put yourself in situations like these? This is the worst thing I can imagine. How do people like this exist?'

King rested his back on the steel mesh. He took a deep breath. 'Over time you come to learn that the whole world is fucked. There's millions of people just like these guys. But I get how it's hard to process.'

'I feel like I'm going to throw up.'

'That's natural.'

'Who are these people?' Burns said, gesturing to the door. 'We were going about our lives in the embassy. They came in and killed all my friends. Took us. We don't know anything.'

'They're a drug gang. They've had this facility for years. No-one knew where it was, but the authorities were getting close to finding it so they did something rash. That's all.'

'Why us?' Norton said from the corner.

'Because that's how the world works. Sometimes normal people like yourselves get put in shit situations like this. And that's why people like me exist. You two might be scared beyond belief but this is normal to me. I've lost count of the amount of times my life has been in danger.'

'You're a genuine madman,' Norton said.

'Maybe.'

'Why do you put yourself in danger?' Burns said. 'You're a smart guy. I'm sure you could have a normal job.'

'I could.'

'Then why?'

'Someone has to do it.'

'It doesn't have to be you.'

King began to explain why it had to be, but was interrupted by the sound of a key turning in a lock behind him. He sprung to his feet as the door swung inward.

Mabaya stepped into the room, brandishing one of the Browning pistols he'd held before. The safety was off.

CHAPTER 25

A palpable tension crept into the room.

Behind him, King heard Norton let out a noise resembling a whimper. The boy shrank further into the corner, like the extra few inches would help him get out of range of Mabaya's gun. A useless effort. One made out of fear. King silently promised he would try and get Norton free even if it meant his own death. This kid didn't deserve to die here.

Up close, he studied Mabaya. The man was a similar height to King. Somewhere around six foot three. Muscle packed his tall frame. His skin glistened with sweat. King wasn't sure if there was a gym in the compound or if the mercenary had excellent genetics. Nevertheless, he was strong. That much was clear. His bald head shone even in the dim lighting. King noted the absence of emotion in his eyes. He was a hard man. A brutal man. Just from the expression in his eyes, King knew he would have no qualms killing the three of them where they stood.

'Hello, American,' Mabaya said, his accent thick. His voice resonated in the small space. Norton flinched at the sound. Burns stood beside King, defiant. She was a strong woman.

'If you let us go, we promise—' Burns began.

Mabaya levelled the Browning at her head. 'Did I say you could speak?'

She fell silent.

'I am talking to this pig,' he said. 'If either you or the pussy boy in the back say a single thing, I will put bullets into you.'

King watched in silence. He made sure to stay completely still, hesitant to move a muscle. Any sudden action would result in his death.

'Now, American,' Mabaya said. 'How did you find us?'

'The police and the government have your location,' he said. 'The local Iquitos police were bringing it to our embassy. That's why you attacked it. You knew they were close.'

'Well then you three are useless to me. I might as well kill you right now.'

'You won't do that.'

'And why is that?'

'I can help you. I know what type of forces we are going to send. I can show you how to escape, because I know exactly how they're going to attack you. You just need to let these two go.'

The barrel of the Browning moved horizontally through the air. It came to a halt aimed directly at King's forehead. He stared death in the eyes. If Mabaya pulled the trigger the small black hole in the centre of the barrel would spit out a bullet and kill him before he even knew what was happening. There would be nothing but instant darkness.

'Do you think I'm a fucking idiot?'

'No.'

'I would rather die than get your help, American. You killed my men. You will die, but not just yet. It will be slow.'

'These two have done nothing to you. I'm the one you have hatred for. Not them.'

'They are Americans. They will die.'

'Please—' Burns started to say.

King knew instantly it was the wrong move. Mabaya's tone had been dead serious when he told her not to speak. He already hated the three of them.

Burns' voice tipped him over the edge.

He shifted his aim once again and pulled the trigger. In the enclosed room the noise exploded off the walls like a detonating bomb. Norton screamed and flinched behind them. The muzzle flash filled King's vision. The next thing he saw was Burns doubling over. Clutching her stomach. Blood began to pour from her mid-section.

She hit the concrete floor with an unceremonious thud and came to rest in the fetal position, hands covering her abdomen. Already her face was deathly pale. Pain creased her features.

King did not hesitate to act. He needed to apply pressure to the wound before she bled out. It might be too late to try, but he couldn't just stand there. He dropped to one knee and hurried to find the exact point of entry of the 9mm bullet.

The wound was significant. Her tattered clothing was already soaked through with blood. King knew he had turned his back to Mabaya. He wouldn't see a bullet coming if the mercenary decided to end his life. But it was his duty to try and save Burns.

'Don't bother,' a voice behind him said.

Another deafening report. King's flinch was involuntary. He'd expected Mabaya to shoot, but he didn't think he would still be alive to hear it. But he hadn't been the target.

Burns' head jerked backward, now sporting a bullet hole in the centre of her forehead. Instantly the life disappeared from her eyes. She was a corpse by the time she came to rest, rolled onto her back by the force of the impact.

It was the final straw. King saw nothing but red. His head filled with blinding, seething rage.

Running off instinct, he turned and charged at the steel mesh. He felt an enormous surge of adrenalin coursing through his veins, lending him speed. His actions were fast. Too fast for Mabaya to get a good aim.

He lashed out with a steel-toed boot, throwing a front kick. A move practiced thousands of times on heavy bags in gyms across the world. Coupled with the burst of primal energy, King struck the flimsy lock in exactly the right spot. The rusting metal bent under the force of the kick, denting beyond repair. As his foot touched the floor he kicked with the other leg. A fluid motion. The movement took no less than a second. This foot struck the centre of the cage door with equal power. It was enough to have its intended effect.

The door tore off its weak hinges. King had guessed correctly when he assumed that the steel mesh had been in place for years. There was limited access to supplies in these parts. It hadn't been designed well enough to withstand such a precise blow. He had expected it to swing open but the material was poorer than even he had anticipated. The entire door flew out of its slot and struck Mabaya. Not enough force to do damage. But he hadn't seen it coming. The impact sent him staggering. One of his boots skidded on the concrete floor and he careered to the floor. The steel mesh landed on him, pinning him awkwardly.

King surged out of the caged area and threw the flimsy door to the side, exposing Mabaya. The incident had taken him by surprise and as a result he had lost his grip on the Browning. It lay by his side, no use to him now.

King thundered an elbow into his throat, once again timing it perfectly. He felt the man's windpipe take a significant impact. He was winded. It was time to finish it. If he had learnt one thing over his career it was that no nobility or honour existed in hand-to-hand combat. In a life or death fight, one must do whatever necessary to ensure their own survival. With that knowledge in his mind he took the opportunity to swing a boot into Mabaya's chin.

He had no idea how much damage the kick had done. It scrambled Mabaya's brain and knocked him senseless. If there was lasting damage, King couldn't care less. The consequences of the kick barely scraped the forefront of his mind. The only thing that mattered was that the man was unconscious.

For a moment he considered the recklessness of his plan. If the door hadn't budged, he would have been shot to pieces. Rage had taken over. Even though he'd come out victorious, he should not have been so careless. Blind luck had been the difference between life and death.

'Jesus Christ,' he heard Norton say from the corner of the room.

The kid would be in shock. Burns — his only companion — was dead. King wasn't sure if Norton had ever seen a corpse before. Coupled with the massive instantaneous violence of the last ten seconds, King didn't blame him for being scared senseless.

'I know this is all too much to process,' he said. 'But you can worry about that later. If you want to live, ignore it and just follow what I do.'

Norton nodded, his eyes wet.

The unconscious body beneath King had a satellite phone attached to its belt. He couldn't help but smile. Now he had exactly what he needed.

'Thank you, Mabaya,' he whispered.

He bent down and snatched the phone out of its holster, scooping up the Browning with his other hand. Ten round magazine. Two rounds were buried in Burns. He had eight bullets.

'Let's go,' he said.

As soon as he spoke, he heard commotion in the hallway. Mabaya had left the door open, revealing a narrow corridor with walls made of aluminium sheeting. The whole place felt shoddily constructed. This area must be a haphazard prison in one corner of the building.

A man rounded the corner. Norton jolted violently, surprised at the sudden encounter. King was ready. He knew the gunshots would have drawn attention. Anticipation was everything in this game. It meant that King took only a fraction of a second to lock his aim onto the bulky figure in the doorway and tap the trigger twice in quick succession.

One in the head, one in the throat. The Phantom was dead before he hit the floor.

'*What the fuck is going on?!*' Norton screamed.

King didn't blame him after witnessing so much death and violence for the first time, but the noise sure was inconvenient. Every mercenary in the compound would be on them in no time. He couldn't hesitate.

'Let's go,' he said again to Norton.

The boy didn't move for a split second. There was no time.

'*Norton, move!*' King roared at the top of his lungs.

It terrified him into action. He scrambled to his feet and followed King into the hallway.

King's eyes darted over his surroundings. He took a quick glance to the left and right. If they went left they would head into the main area of the compound. A large warehouse, King guessed. Most of the Phantoms would be scattered around the room. If he was alone, it would be his path of choice. He wasn't one to run from a fight, and right now he had the biggest advantage of them all. Surprise. If he didn't have Norton in his company, he would hunt down and kill every last remaining Phantom. That was his nature.

But it carried a level of risk that he was not willing to expose the boy to. Norton deserved safety. He deserved every ounce of help King could give. And that meant escape.

The other end of the corridor ran into the edge of the building. A window sat at chest-height, built into the smooth concrete wall. Just large enough to fit through. It led onto the rear of the compound, which consisted of a small open clearing surrounded by dense jungle. That was where they would head.

'Out that window, okay?' King said. 'Go smash it.'

'What?'

'Go break the glass. I'll keep you covered.'

'Uh…'

'Norton, for fuck's sakes, go. I'm going to make sure you don't die. Hurry up.'

The boy made for the end of the hallway. King dropped to one knee and aimed the Browning in the other direction, ready for anyone who dared to come through.

He heard shouting out in the main area. It echoed off the walls and the high ceiling. They knew there was trouble. They would come charging in any second.

He heard Norton smash the window, but he kept his gaze locked. Any second…

He saw a flash of movement. He spammed the trigger three times, more reflex than measured accuracy. Nevertheless, it was enough. Two bullets hit the Phantom who came charging into the hallway and he skidded face-first across the floor, carried by his own momentum. The gun in his hands came free and clattered along the concrete, coming to rest near King.

A Taurus PT92 pistol. Probably fully loaded. They had a fifteen round magazine.

He'd take it.

With his free hand he switched the Browning for the Taurus and bolted for the window. Norton was halfway out. He knew the other Phantoms would hesitate to enter as brazenly as their friend, who had died for his brashness. He had maybe a few seconds.

He was a foot away from the window when he heard the cock of an automatic weapon from far behind.

Wrong. They weren't hesitating.

He threw himself at the window with everything he had. Pure nerves lent him another much-needed burst of energy. His torso exited the window first, followed by his legs. One thigh scraped along the broken glass, drawing blood. It was the least of his concerns. As he crash-landed in the mud, several rounds flew over his head, chasing him out the window. They'd missed by inches.

Norton lay prone on the clearing floor. His legs shook uncontrollably. He was a nervous wreck.

King sprung to his knees, raised the hand with the Taurus in it and fired three rounds blindly through the broken window.

The gunfire stopped. The Phantoms had ducked for cover inside. Now was their one and only chance to get clear of the compound.

He made a beeline for the jungle. On the way, he reached down and scooped Norton up with one hand, throwing him to his feet. It spurred the boy into action. Together they flew across the clearing and crashed into the foliage, disappearing into the trees before the remaining Phantoms had a chance to shoot them down.

CHAPTER 26

For a minute straight, they ran in silence. Norton had lost all disregard for injury. Every atom of his being was focused on survival. King had seen it before in newcomers to a warzone. Every type of injury lost all meaning. Staying alive was the only priority. The boy powered through the rainforest, almost turning his ankle over several times.

King reached out a hand and grabbed Norton's shoulder. He jumped.

'That's it, kid,' he said. 'We're far enough away. Take your time.'

Even with a loose grip, King felt the boy shaking.

'Let's go!' Norton said. 'Let's go, come on, let's go!'

'Don't rush. You'll break your ankle and then I'll have to carry you. And then they might catch us.'

'Okay.'

He slowed significantly after that. They jogged for another hundred feet, putting distance between themselves and the compound. Then King stopped Norton again.

'That's far enough.'

'What do you mean that's far enough?! Let's get the fuck out of here!'

'No, because then we'll get lost. And then all the running in the world won't mean shit. We'll die of thirst or starvation. I'd almost rather take a bullet.'

Norton saw the satellite phone in his hand.

'Do you know how to use that?'

'It's a satellite phone,' King said. 'Pretty basic military appliance. I think I'm good.'

'So you can call for backup?'

'I can.'

Then Norton did something that took King by surprise. He wrapped his arms around his shoulders and hugged him.

'Thank you for saving my life,' he muttered.

King took a moment to process it. He lived his life on the battlefield. Gestures such as these were few and far between. He paused for a second, then reached up and ruffled the kid's hair.

'No problem, buddy. It's what I do.'

They parted.

'Time to get out of here?'

'You bet.'

They found a small alcove in between two trees and hunched down into it, away from prying eyes. King fiddled with the satellite phone, thumbing its buttons until he found what he needed. He dialled in a memorised number and let it ring.

It was answered on the second.

'Name?' a female voice said.

'Jason King.'

'Confirm, please.'

'Arctic two chopper, zero three warthog.' The people on the other end of the line were the only others who knew his identification code. It protected them from falling for any kind of impersonation.

'Putting you through now.'

A few moments of static, then another voice came on, this one male.

'This is Lars.'

'Lars, it's King.'

Lars Crawford held more power than any of the other Joint Chiefs of Staff, yet he technically did not exist. No records were kept of his dealings. He held no official government title. He worked from deep inside the Pentagon, often advising the Chairman of the Joint Chiefs, the man considered the most senior military official in the country.

Mostly, he ran Black Force.

King worked under the command of Black Force. No-one knew who they were, for good reason. Their forces consisted of only a few men, hand-picked from either Delta or DEVGRU. They were allowed to attempt what any official entity would write off as impossible, because they did not exist to any official entity. It gave them absolute discretion. They were men who had devoted their entire lives to the military. King did not know the others. He showed up, completed a mission and collected his paycheque. Because they had no books, Black Force paid handsomely. And it was all run by Lars Crawford, a brilliant mind who had been deemed too valuable to remain in his position as Sergeant Major of the Marine Corps. His work was stellar, but he often overstepped the line. So the President took him off the record and gave him his own office away from prying eyes. Where he could accomplish great things that no-one would ever know about.

According to documentation he had retired to Wisconsin after leaving the Marine Corps.

'Where the fuck have you been?' he said. 'You disappeared, for fuck's sakes. Delta's currently cleaning up the airfield you left, trying to piece together where you went.'

'I continued with the mission,' King said. 'I have one of them with me. Ben Norton. The other two are dead. They'd all be dead if I had waited. I need extraction, but there's still a few hostiles left in the compound.'

'There's four Delta boys at the airfield. They have a CH-53.'

'A Super Stallion?'

'Yeah. I managed to secure one. It'll help.'

'It's getting dark. Wait until morning. There's no point losing any men by rushing it.'

'Do you have supplies?'

'No. But we'll manage.'

'Are you hurt?'

King looked down at himself. The relentless pace of his time awake had caused him to ignore his injuries. Now, he studied them. The glue in his wrist had dried solid. He could use his hand, meaning that there was no significant nerve damage. The taut bandage around his shoulder was soaked through with blood, but once again he still had function. In pain, yes. But not paralysed. He would make it through another day.

'I'm fine,' he said.

'How's the hostage? Files say he's nineteen.'

'He'll survive.'

'Okay. They'll arrive at 0700. We have your position from the GPS on the phone you're using. Is that the exact place you want extraction?'

'Come to this exact location and find the clearest place to land. If Delta has a Super Stallion, we'll hear it from a mile away.'

'Good luck, King.'

He hung up. No wasted words. Nothing unnecessary said. Just what needed to be done, and how long it would take. Conversations with Lars were nothing but efficient.

They had talked on loudspeaker, so Norton had heard the whole thing. For a moment, the boy smiled. A rare expression in a time like this.

'I didn't think I would make it out of there,' he said.

King began to speak, but a strange emotion sent a pang through his chest.

The feeling of regret.

He bowed his head into his hands and tried his hardest not to cry. Frustration swelled inside him. He felt Norton rest a hand on his shoulder.

'Um, Mr. King, are you okay?'

He nodded. 'I think I fucked this one up, Ben.'

'How?'

'I shouldn't have come here. Two of you are dead. If we'd just waited, maybe things would have been different.'

'You didn't fuck anything up,' Norton said. 'If you'd waited any longer, they would have done things to us that they were waiting to do. Mabaya said that some of them wanted to...' He trailed off. 'You know, I didn't think there was that much savagery in the world.'

'You just haven't seen it before.'

'I've studied it. We have all sorts of theories on terrorism and crime in international relations. I just … never thought about what it would actually look like. I'm sheltered, I guess.'

King shook his head. 'You're normal. Not many people choose to confront that stuff their whole lives.'

'It must take a toll.'

He shrugged. 'I can deal with it, mostly. I'd rather be in these situations and seeing these things and helping people than ignoring what's happening and letting them die. That's why I do what I do.'

'I could never do that.'

'Not many people could.'

It was almost fully dark. King couldn't see the sun dip below the horizon, but the sky melted from an incandescent orange to a stark grey. The jungle seemed to come alive around this time. The noise of wildlife echoed all around them. Birds hooting, insects buzzing. Somewhere in the distance, water flowed.

'Should we head further out?' Norton said.

'I don't think—'

A few dozen feet behind the alcove, a cacophony of shouting rose up. Two sharp discharges exploded, resonating off the trees. A spray of wild bullets passed over their heads.

'Yes, I think we should,' King said.

They took off into the night.

CHAPTER 27

Despite the panic of fleeing enemy gunfire, King knew he had to make sure not to grow careless. If he and Norton got lost, no amount of backup would ever save them. The Amazon Rainforest was so vast and unexplored that losing their way would mean a death sentence.

As they ran, King used his good arm to break low-hanging branches. The snapped twigs fell to the forest floor beneath them. It would serve as a rudimentary path back should they need it.

The darkness became an advantage to them. Slowly, the sounds of the remaining Phantoms grew quieter and quieter. When King noticed this he grabbed Norton once again and stood deathly still, listening intently.

The noise began to fade.

'They lost us,' he said. 'We're good.'

The Amazon at night was a different beast. Keeping track of his location was hard enough with the assistance of daylight, but now it was practically impossible. King found himself surrounded by looming trees, all resembling each other. He could barely remember which direction led back to the compound.

'We should bunker down here,' he said. 'Get some sleep. They won't spend much more time searching. It'll be useless when it's fully dark.'

There was no camp to set up, for they had no supplies on them. King's backpack was a mile away, tucked away somewhere in the dark jungle on the other side of the compound. He would never find it, at least until morning. Even then it would be tough to locate.

They found the most comfortable patch of ground and lay down amongst the ferns. After the chaos of the day, King would take any rest he could. He didn't care about a fire, or a good meal, or clean drinking water. He just wanted to avoid being shot at for a few hours.

'I'm scared, King,' Norton said after a lengthy period of silence.

King paused. He could hear unsuppressed fear in the kid's voice. He didn't blame him. To Norton, their current predicament would be unfathomable. Just a few days ago all the kid had known was the inside of an embassy, and the worst of his worries had probably been what job offerings would result from an internship in Peru. Now he lay buried in the cover of jungle undergrowth, heart pounding in his chest, sweat on his brow, praying desperately that merciless gangsters didn't find him and kill him … or worse.

'I am too,' King said. 'Believe me.'

'There's no way! You said you want to be in these situations. Can you teach me how? I can't handle this.'

'It's not something you can teach, kid. It's not as simple as that. I started just as nervous as you are. Over time you can learn to suppress it. But it never really goes away.'

'How did you end up volunteering for missions like this…?' Norton said. Then he waited, as if hesitant to ask a question that he didn't want to come off as rude.

'Say it,' King said. 'I won't mind.'

'Did you come from a bad home?'

King chuckled. 'It would make sense if I did, wouldn't it? An orphan, thrown around foster care. That'd explain my decision perfectly.'

'You didn't?'

'Quite the opposite. I was two years into a law degree when I decided to sign up for the military. And my goal was to become someone like this.'

'W—' Norton didn't have a response to that.

'Don't worry. You wouldn't be the first not to understand. In fact, it'd be strange if you did understand.'

'This isn't natural,' Norton said. 'Wouldn't you prefer not having to worry about whether you'll see the next day?'

'Not really. I thrive on that feeling.'

'How? Because right now my instincts are telling me to curl up into a ball and cry and wait for it to all be over.'

'I don't have an exact answer. I never will. I get energy from the thrill of near-death experiences. I only feel like I'm alive when I'm scared.'

'So it's not about helping people?'

'It is. But everyone cares about their own life, too. If you don't, you're a liar. I just happen to be impartial to danger, so I can do what I do without a second thought.'

'I don't get it.'

'Then you won't get what I'm going to do tomorrow morning.'

He heard Norton sit up in the dark. 'Please don't say...'

'I'm going back there, kid. I left Mabaya alive. And there's still five or six Phantoms, somewhere out there.'

'Can't we just run? Please?'

'If I die, you just hunker down and wait for the sound of the chopper. The backup is arriving in a CH-53 Super Stallion, so you'll hear it from a mile away. Largest chopper in the United States military.'

'Can't they take care of the men left in that place?'

'They could, but I don't want to risk any casualties on their end. I'm the one who chose to proceed with the mission. I don't care if I die. I care if they do.'

Norton said nothing for a while. In the far distance, the faint echo of barking commands crept through the jungle.

Mabaya's awake, King thought. *And mad as hell.*

'I still don't get it,' Norton said. 'But please promise me I'm going to be okay.'

'You'll be fine,' King said. 'I can't say the same for myself.'

'Why can't you just forget about it?'

'If I do nothing … and one of the Delta soldiers gets killed in the firefight…' He shook his head. 'I couldn't live with myself.'

'It's not your responsibility.'

'I know. But I'm making it mine. I *want* to.'

'But—'

'You won't change my mind, Ben.'

They lay on the jungle floor in mutual silence, listening to the sounds of the Amazon all around them. Incessant shrieking and hooting and hollering of wildlife disturbed the quiet, making King restless. He rolled onto his side and grimaced. The rest gave him time to concentrate on his injuries. To feel the throbbing pain in his wrist. To feel the nerve endings tweaking in his shoulder. He longed for another burst of adrenaline. That feeling melted away all others. There was nothing to concentrate on but the heat of combat.

I must be sick, he thought. Maybe he was. Norton was right. This wasn't how normal people lived. In the darkness, he shrugged. As long as he could save people like Norton in the process, he didn't care if he was different. Sometimes, different was a benefit.

He felt the stock of the Taurus PT92. It calmed him a little. There were twelve bullets left in the chamber. He'd fired three through the compound's window when they were escaping.

There was a lot he could do with twelve bullets. The Phantoms would find out how much in the morning.

Once again, King found himself thinking about death. What if he was killed in battle tomorrow morning? He imagined the scenario, and waited for his brain to respond. Some kind of feeling, some kind of worry.

Nothing.

That in itself was worrying. He did not care whether he lived or died tomorrow.

'Norton, you awake?' he said.

Silence.

In the relative comfort of the foliage, the kid had crashed. King didn't blame him. Twenty-four hours of constant tension would do that. In a moment of relative safety, he'd fallen instantly asleep. King could feel the same effect beginning to affect himself. He reached for the digital watch on his wrist and thumbed the buttons on one side of its bulk. Three beeps told him what he needed to know. There was an alarm set for five in the morning. He knew he didn't need it, but it was precautionary.

He settled back into the fronds, letting them wrap around him. He thought he felt a bug crawl across his earlobe. He flitted it away and winced at the searing pain in his shoulder. What if he woke up unable to move his arm?

He would worry about that in the morning. He closed his eyes and felt the murky haze of sleep take over.

CHAPTER 28

His eyes flitted open seconds before the alarm went off. A strange phenomenon, and one that he couldn't easily explain. His brain seemed to sense when combat was imminent. When he wasn't on a mission, he never woke up when he wanted.

It was still dark, but not the kind of jet-black that came in the middle of the night. A faint sliver of blue crept into the sky above. King looked up at the trees overhead and could make out the outline of the branches against the sky. There was just enough light to navigate around. Which is exactly what he would need to do.

His heart rate ever so slowly began to quicken. A feeling he would never get tired of. As he got to his feet, Norton stirred beside him.

'Are you leaving?'

King nodded. 'Afraid I am.'

'What do I do?'

'Do what I told you. Wait for me to come back. If I don't, just stay here. Backup will arrive in exactly two hours. Delta is never late. No matter what happens you'll be safe. I promise.'

'Thank you, King. I'd be dead if it wasn't for you.'

'Happy to help. You know why.'

King gripped Norton's shoulder with his good hand and squeezed tight. 'You'll be fine.'

'I'd prefer if you didn't die in the next two hours. I thought we would be friends.'

King smiled. 'I'll try not to.'

He tucked the Taurus into his belt, turned and headed into the trees.

As he walked, he did his best to ignore his wounds. Medical assistance would be there in hours. He had to keep the pain at bay long enough to achieve his objective, then he could let it consume him. Until then...

His first destination was the river. There was something he needed there. Just enough light had crept into the sky to make the path ahead faintly visible. It enabled him to skirt around obstacles, avoiding fallen logs and dips in the ground and twisting roots. His surroundings made claustrophobia inevitable. No matter how resolutely King acted, it was impossible to shake the knot in his gut. The fear that he would get lost and slowly succumb to dehydration.

He need not have worried. His sense of direction was impeccable. It took less than ten minutes before he saw the riverbank ahead, sloping away from the jungle. He exited the rainforest and took a moment to watch the river.

Although light had begun to creep over the horizon, moonlight still shone across the water. He saw the flowing streams pulsate slightly, spurred on by the slope of the land. It was a serene sight. He knew the calm wouldn't last long.

He had a job to do.

Down by the shore tiny waves lapped at the dirt, creating a stretch of mud that ran for miles in either direction. King crept down to the water, taking caution not to slip. After being shot twice, he was in enough trouble already. Impaired movement was the last thing he wanted to add to that.

In the dawn light he scooped out a thick dollop of mud and smeared it over his neck. With both hands he spread the cold gunk over his cheeks, his forehead, his chin. He ran it through his hair. He covered his exposed arm, missing the sleeve that was now tied tight around the wound in his shoulder. By the time he was finished and the mud had caked dry against his skin, all his exposed flesh was entirely brown. It would blend him into the undergrowth.

They'd never see him coming.

He withdrew the Taurus from his waistband and clicked the safety off. It was a sound ingrained into his memory. It always signified impending pain and death and destruction. The pre-eminent noise of approaching combat. It helped him enter a dark place, a place he knew he had to go to achieve what he wanted. At the compound there could be no hesitation. He couldn't stop to think about what he was doing. Gunfights were instinctive. There would be no mercy from either side.

He snuck back into the jungle and let the dense vegetation envelop him. He felt invisible, and he knew he would be hard to spot. It took him five minutes to find the compound. At first he thought he never would. All the trees blurred into one another, until it felt like he was walking through a kaleidoscope of green. He wasn't sure he would ever find his way, until the trees cleared ahead and he saw the outline of the warehouse in the distance.

He dropped to his stomach and crept slowly toward the compound. Amongst the ferns he was a ghost. They would not see him until it was too late. He saw movement in his peripheral vision and stopped crawling. There were three men on this side of the clearing. They patrolled the ground between the main warehouse and the jungle in a haphazard, predictable fashion. Clearly untrained. King smiled and silently thanked Mabaya for failing to train his men properly.

As if on cue, the man himself rounded the corner of the warehouse. The right side of his face had incipient swelling, with splotches of purple dotted across his cheek.

An after-effect of King's boot.

The three gangsters turned to their leader, all facing away from King. Now would be the opportune time to strike, but he did not yet have a proper read on the situation. He would wait a little longer. Observe and assess.

'Any sign of him?' Mabaya said in Spanish.

'The fucker is long gone,' one of the goons snarled.

'Maybe. I have a feeling he's coming back. We'll kill him when he does.'

'He has to,' the second man said. 'They'll die out there. We're the only resources around.'

'I don't know,' Mabaya said, staring away. 'He took my fucking phone.'

'He what?'

'The satellite phone. The Garmin. He took it when he attacked me.'

The third Phantom, who up until then had been silent, let out an outburst. 'Why didn't you tell us that before?! There's going to be military coming here. We need to leave. You dumb *fuck*, Mabaya!'

King watched the exchange with fascination. Mabaya would not have reacted kindly to that tone from one of his underlings a couple of days ago. Just yesterday, he had exuded the authority of a man in undoubtable control of his men.

Now, he simply shrugged.

Nonchalant. Defeated.

'We have to hope he comes back,' Mabaya said. 'It's our only chance. Otherwise we're dead, no matter what.'

He pivoted on his heel and walked back the way he'd come. The three Phantoms patrolling this side of the compound began to shift from foot to foot. King could see they were nervous.

He glanced over his surroundings. If he could get into the warehouse without detection, it would be simple enough to put the remaining Phantoms on the back foot. He could cause a great deal of chaos in a short space of time. Which was exactly what he needed to gain the upper hand. If he tried an attack now, he wouldn't last five seconds. All three of the Phantoms brandished various Kalashnikov rifles. All infinitely more powerful than King's Taurus.

If he wanted to win this, he had to outsmart them.

A large tree next to him rested in a precarious position. He took one look at it and knew it was unstable. The tree's roots had erupted from the dirt days ago, whether from rainy conditions or some other means. Now it had begun to tilt. Its branches and the top of its trunk rested against a neighbouring tree, tentatively balanced. At some point, it would slide off and come crashing to the forest floor.

King wondered if he could make that happen sooner rather than later.

He waited patiently for the three sentries to break their pattern. It didn't take long. Amateurs made mistakes, and these men were the definition of novices. There was little competition in the middle of the jungle. They were rusty. Sure enough, only a few minutes later two of them had their backs turned, smoking cigarettes, while the other peered out into the bushes in the opposite direction of King. There were no eyes on him.

He rose out of the undergrowth and made for the tree. Its trunk was smooth, weathered by the elements over the years. He placed both hands on it and pushed hard. A slight shift. Not enough. He dropped his shoulder low and rammed his frame into the tree, giving it everything he had.

The tree creaked. Overhead he heard a branch snap as it began to slide off its resting position. Any second it would break free.

He let go and raced through the jungle, sticking to the areas packed with vegetation. Hoping to stay away from prying eyes. He made sure to stay close to the compound, circling around its perimeter until he came to a stop near the other side.

The front of the compound had a wider clearing. The same area Woodford had met his demise half a day earlier. Here, four more Phantoms stood idly in the lowlight, glancing nervously in all directions. They hadn't seen King get into position. He knew they wouldn't be around for long.

A deep, booming crash resonated through the ground, coming from the rear of the warehouse. The tree trunk slamming against the dirt created more commotion than King could have hoped for. Mabaya came sprinting out of the warehouse, shouting incoherently. The four Phantoms followed him around the side. Another rookie mistake. There was no need for eight men to investigate a single noise. It left them exposed.

Exactly how King had planned it.

He broke out onto open ground. The clearing was now empty. There was no-one around to stop him as he raced across the dirt and ducked inside the warehouse.

CHAPTER 29

The interior of the warehouse was foreign to King. He'd been carried through it while unconscious, and had yet to see it in the flesh. All he'd glimpsed was a dirty windowless room and a narrow hallway.

The far wall held a mountainous set of steel-framed storage shelves, home to all kinds of plastic-wrapped materials. There had to be enough ingredients for hundreds of kilograms of drugs on the shelves alone. The floor was covered in rows of machinery, all heavy and steel and industrial. All organised to perfection. There were no men in lab coats producing the cocaine. No hired help. King realised the Phantoms manufactured the supply themselves. They were sloppy in combat because this took up the majority of their time.

One table stood out from the rest. Most shone under the halogen lights far above, polished and scrubbed until they were spotless. One was covered in blood.

King crossed the room and approached the table slick with red. On it lay a single object.

Roman Woodford's head.

It had been brutally hacked off his shoulders. The body was nowhere to be seen. His head lay propped up on the table, surrounded by thick droplets of blood. Eyes still wide open. King shook his head at the savagery. He took one more look at Mabaya's sick trophy before moving on. There was work to be done, and no time to dwell on what had already happened. He would not go searching for Burns' head. She was dead. There was nothing more he could do but avenge her.

King made his way over to the shelving. It towered above him, reaching high toward the roof, almost touching the steel beams criss-crossing overhead. The supplies rested in timber cartons. Perfect for setting alight.

He found what he was looking for next to a discarded outboard motor. King guessed it came from one of the boats he had used yesterday. Adjacent to it lay a fat canister of fuel, full to the brim. He wrapped his good hand around the plastic handle and lifted. The fuel was heavy, but motivation lent him strength. He upended its contents over one of the lower shelves, soaking most of the wood. Next he retrieved a blowtorch from the nearest workstation and fired it up.

This will draw some attention.

He threw the lit blowtorch onto the bottom shelf.

As soon as the blue flame touched the puddle of fuel the whole area caught alight. Even as he retreated, King felt the heat searing his back. It spread faster than he thought possible. Within half a minute the far side of the warehouse roared with flames, fuelled by the heat of the warehouse and the mountains of timber.

King took cover behind one of the steel countertops. He knew what was coming. Someone would come running in, surprised at the sudden turn of events, unsure of what was happening.

In fact, it was two men.

A pair of Phantoms were the first to arrive at the scene. From a narrow crack between the tables, King watched their faces fall as they hurried through the doorway and gazed upon their destroyed supplies.

He burst out of cover and fired a pair of shots from the Taurus before they had time to realise he was there. One caught the man on the left in the chest and the other hit home, sending a bullet between the second man's eyes and tumbling into his brain. He was killed instantly. The chest shot probably did the trick also, but King made sure by taking a step forward and finishing the first guy off with a quick headshot.

Twelve bullets left.

Six men left.

The others would be smarter. Mabaya would be directing them, and it seemed he was the only man in their gang with combat training. King snuck up to the doorframe …

… and fell back as a volley of shots pinged through into the concrete.

They were ready for him.

Suddenly, he realised his mistake.

Mabaya had effectively capitalised on the situation by surrounding the main entrance with his men. The warehouse had become stifling from the inferno on its far wall. King felt sweat dripping off his face, splattering the dusty concrete beneath him. If he didn't get out of here soon, he would either burn to death or suffocate from the smoke. He hadn't anticipated that Mabaya would surround the building so quickly. Now he was trapped.

He fired three shots out the open door, and the gunfire ceased momentarily. It wouldn't be enough. As soon as he stepped out onto open ground he would be torn to pieces by automatic gunfire.

Nine bullets left, a voice reminded him.

Leaving through the front door was no longer an option. King turned and started with shock as he saw the blaze eating away at the workstations, lighting instruments and material on fire. The air grew thick and heavy. Smoke cascaded down from the roof, surrounding him. He had perhaps thirty seconds to move.

There were no windows. No way to escape.

The hallway.

He looked for the sub-section of the warehouse. There it was in the far corner, already shrouded in black smoke. Flames licked at its timber walls. It was his only chance of getting out.

He took off at a sprint, darting between countertops and twisting machinery. As he ran he watched the flames begin to swallow the entire area. It didn't matter. He would have to run straight through them if he wanted any chance at survival.

The entrance to the hallway still lay open. A tongue of fire licked across the ground in front of the door. King pumped his legs harder and flew across the fiery surface, feeling a slight twinge as the flames seared his khakis. Thankfully, they didn't catch alight. The mud he'd smeared earlier served as a temporary flame repellent, just enough for him to pass through without burning alive.

Now he was in the hallway, his face beet red. It felt like a furnace inside the narrow room, but King ignored it and kept running. The pain was unbearable, but if he did not push through it he would die. He felt the searing blaze eat away at the material all around him. He saw the window at the end, still broken. He wondered if it was being guarded. He dismissed that thought. A bullet in the brain was preferable to being burnt alive.

Five more steps.

The flames licked at his back.

Four.

He felt them consume him.

He jumped with three steps left.

It was an all-or-nothing move, a leap of faith that he hoped had enough momentum behind it to send him through the window. Surrounded by fire he passed through the small opening, missing the ledge by inches. Then, just like that, he was out. He hit the cool mud outside on his back and rolled to his feet, still shocked by how close he had come to death. He looked back at where he had come from and saw the hallway was nothing but a blazing inferno. The entire warehouse had been consumed by flames.

A shot rang past his ear.

He spun again and rolled to the side, creating distance from his last position. An instinctive motion. Throwing off whoever was shooting at him. As he gathered his wits he saw a Phantom out of the corner of his eye. Just one man. Aiming a handgun at him. His eyes were wide, his complexion undeniably startled. He hadn't expected King to come through the window, especially followed by flames. He'd had one chance to put him away and he'd failed.

King levelled his Taurus and shot twice. He didn't even have time to see where he hit the Phantom, but the man dropped regardless. Out of the equation. Either injured or dead. It didn't matter which.

He turned and made for the trees as fast as humanly possible. It wouldn't be long before they were all on him. He had seven bullets left. It wasn't enough.

As he powered into the foliage once again, he heard a familiar sound nearby. The booming, ear-splitting throbbing of helicopter blades. And not just any helicopter blades.

The CH-53E Super Stallion had a distinctive sound that King had come to memorise over his years of service. It sounded unlike any other chopper in the U.S. military. It was the largest, the heaviest and the most powerful behemoth in the armed forces. You could hear one coming from miles away.

He checked his watch. 0620. The sun had yet to fully rise.

The Delta Force soldiers were early. Very early. Nevertheless, he welcomed their presence. His lungs ached and his skin tingled from the close call in the warehouse and his shoulder burned and his wounded wrist was numb.

It was time to get out of the jungle.

CHAPTER 30

The Super Stallion came into view, a glorious sight amidst the carnage.

Its massive rotor blades span faster than the eye could see. Its bulk roared over the treetops and came to a halt above the clearing, hovering effortlessly.

Instantly, shots from the Phantoms on the far side of the warehouse pinged off its hull. It stayed in place. Kalashnikov bullets were nothing but toothpicks against its bulletproof undercarriage.

From its position above the warehouse, King made eye contact with the pilot. He saw the hesitation in the man's face. The warehouse was now fully ablaze. There was no clear area to land, apart from directly on top of the remaining Phantoms. That was doable, but it would most likely result in a friendly casualty or two.

Something King was determined to avoid.

He waved an arm in the direction of where he'd left Norton, instructing the pilot to find somewhere else to land.

That way, Norton could follow the sound of the rotors until he happened upon its landing zone. King would find them later.

He had unfinished business.

With a curt nod, the pilot ascended and powered the Super Stallion directly over King, heading toward Norton's last known position. The kid was safe, at least. His work with Norton was done.

Now ... he would kill Mabaya.

As the almighty drone of the chopper faded into the distance, King burrowed down into the fronds once more. Hopefully for the last time.

It didn't take long for the last four Phantoms to enter his sight. They rounded the corner of the blazing warehouse in a tight-knit group. Panic creased their faces. There was no sign of Mabaya. Their leader gone, their compound ablaze, their supplies destroyed.

They were stranded in the heart of an inhospitable jungle, hunted by an American they thought had been defeated when they'd captured him. Now they seemed terrified, a feeling that had caused them to cluster together.

Like shooting fish in a barrel, King thought.

He raised the Taurus, but something stopped him. A noise in the bushes behind him. Someone crashing through the jungle. He spun fast, but there was no-one there. Just endless rows of trees, now lit by the rising sun creeping through the branches above, casting a golden glow over everything. He turned back. Swore under his breath. Realising he had missed his opportunity.

The four men fanned out into the clearing, now ten paces away from each other, weapons raised. He would never be able to put them all down without exposing his position and leaving himself completely open to returning automatic gunfire.

Gut tightening, he realised one was getting close. So close, in fact, that he couldn't move without highlighting his position in the bushes. The man had a slight frame, around five foot nine and skinny. He was not the problem. The AK-74 in his hands was the problem. It would only take a quick pull of the trigger to send King into oblivion. He didn't dare move.

The Phantom was looking away, for now. He took another step, so close he was within touching distance. King decided it was time to act. Otherwise, he risked getting shot to pieces.

He leapt to his feet, less than two feet in front of the Phantom. The man jolted so violently that the aim of the AK-74 strayed to the side. King used the moment of surprise to his advantage, knocking the gun away and wrapping his other arm around the man's neck. With one swift motion, he dragged him down into the bushes.

The burning warehouse let out a deafening racket, which meant that the other three Phantoms hadn't heard a thing. King burrowed deep into the vegetation and squeezed with every ounce of power in his arm, choking the Phantom into unconsciousness, a burly forearm tight across his throat. It only took ten seconds. He made sure the man was out, then released his grip.

The other three had no idea. They were switching between staring at the burning warehouse and gazing far off into the jungle, searching for nothing in particular.

King knew utter demoralisation when he saw it. They had certainly not expected their day to turn out like this. Even if they managed to kill him, and all the reinforcements coming in his wake, they were still screwed. No supplies. No means of contacting whatever friends they may have in Iquitos.

King knew he was looking at broken men.

For a moment he thought about leaving them be, but decided against it. They would either run off into the jungle and die a slower, more painful death. Or they would choose to stand and fight the Delta Force soldiers, perhaps resulting in a casualty or two. Either option was less ideal than a bullet in the brain.

He would give them that.

He lined up the Taurus' aim at the nearest Phantom and let out a long exhale. Calming himself down. Letting his hands become still. It would do no good to miss the mark and cause any additional pain than was necessary. He wanted his shot to put the lights out.

Then something happened he wasn't expecting.

The Phantom's gaze darted over and spotted King instantly. The two men froze, making eye contact.

Before King could pull the trigger, the Phantom brought his AK-74 up and unleashed the magazine in his direction, screaming simultaneously.

King fell back into the shrubs as bullets tore up the ground around him. As he dove for cover, he let two rounds fly.

One missed.

The other punctured the Phantom in the stomach and he dropped to his knees, still roaring at the top of his lungs.

Now the other two were onto him.

'Fuck,' King whispered, his heart racing.

He had to do something right now, to stop the Phantoms shooting him to shit. Gritting his teeth in panic, he fired the Taurus in all directions until it clicked dry. He didn't hit anything but the pair ducked instinctively, delaying their gunfire.

As the Taurus' magazine clicked dry King knew he had to flee. There were no other options. He'd had ample chances to finish off the last remaining Phantoms, and he'd blown it. With regret and fear coursing through his body he spun on one heel, frantic, and ran off in the direction he'd seen the Super Stallion head.

With cries of bloodlust, the two non-injured Phantoms gave pursuit.

CHAPTER 31

For as long as he lived, King would never grow used to the feeling of running for his life.

It was unbearable. He had no time to throw a glance behind him, so he could do nothing but presume that he was being followed. Every step he took he expected to feel a bullet hit him in the back. Or the head. If it hit him there, would he even feel it? Or would there just be sudden darkness? The unknown of the situation terrified him. When he could face his enemies, he was able to remain calm. Whatever happened, he would see it coming.

But this was hell.

A shot whisked past his ear, so close he could feel it. It thwacked into a nearby tree, puncturing the wood to splinters. He zigzagged, taking wild lateral movements in an attempt to throw off the aim of his pursuers. It worked well enough. Another few rounds passed him by, but these were much further from their mark. The disadvantage of chasing someone with an assault rifle was that if you wanted any hope of hitting them, you had to stop and take aim. Handguns could be fired on the move. AK-74s couldn't, unless they were spray-and-praying, which would do nothing. Every time they paused to fire off a volley of shots, King increased the distance between them.

By the time he made it back to Norton, he'd carved out a sizeable lead.

'King!' Norton cried. 'I thought—'

'Ben, let's fucking move!' King roared as he closed in on the small inlet, legs still pumping. 'Right now! Did you hear the chopper?'

'Yeah, it went that way but I wanted to wait for y—'

'Here I am. Let's go!'

'What's going on?'

'*Now!*'

To demonstrate his urgency, another cluster of AK-47 rounds burst through the trees to their left.

'Oh, fuck!' Norton cried.

The pair bolted in the opposite direction to the compound, away from the last Phantoms giving chase. Now there was no time to worry about turning ankles. They couldn't slow down. If they did, King knew they would get hit. He only had to give the Phantoms one decent chance to aim and they would capitalise on it.

The further they ran, the thicker the jungle seemed to grow. King didn't often get claustrophobic, but the jungle seemed to draw it from his bones. As he squeezed through narrow gaps between tree trunks and powered through low-hanging branches and knocked aside overgrown ferns he found his chest constricting. Fear reared its ugly head, sending a shiver down his spine. If they got stuck...

He couldn't imagine how Norton was feeling. The kid ran behind him, waiting as King muscled a path through the jungle, his breath heavy and thick with fear. King thought he heard a sob at one point, but he ignored it. There was all the time in the world to worry about Norton's state of mind later. First he had to get the kid out of these parts alive.

The noise of the Super Stallion grew louder. The incessant *thwack-thwack-thwack* of the rotors was now coming from somewhere directly ahead. Not from the sky.

'They've landed somewhere,' King told Norton. 'Hurry.'

The pair burst out into a large clearing, almost the same size as the Phantoms' compound. The Super Stallion sat in the centre of the flat area, rotors still spinning full-blast, wheels perched on the clearing floor. Its tail faced toward them, the rear rotor pulsating, sending waves of wind rippling their clothes.

King grabbed Norton's shirt to make sure he stayed behind him and didn't venture too close to the chopper's blades. He set off across the clearing...

... and the Super Stallion took off.

King watched in disbelief as it rose off the clearing floor and began to hover above the treetops, sending a mighty downdraft billowing into the clearing. The wind almost knocked King off his feet. It battered him like an invisible fist. In the confusion he let go of Norton's shirt and the slight boy clattered to the dirt, unable to withstand the power of the downdraft. The chopper dipped its nose and headed further south of the Phantoms' compound, passing over the trees and disappearing from sight. The din faded once more.

Once voices were audible, Norton swore in disgust.

'What the fuck was that?' he said. 'Where are they going?'

'Maybe they thought we were Phantoms. I'm covered in mud. There's nothing to clearly signify that I'm a friendly.'

'They were right there...' Norton's voice quaked as he realised how close they had come to rescue.

'Don't worry,' King said, even though worry had begun to creep into his own mind. Something wasn't right, but appearances were everything. He had to calm Norton down. 'We'll meet them further along. Follow me.'

He took off running again. There was no time to waste. In seconds the men pursuing them would reach the clearing.

Then there would be nothing but a wide open shot between their barrels and King's head. He couldn't let that happen.

They reached the far side of the clearing just as shouts rose from where they had come. King knew what was coming. He reached back, wrapped a hand around Norton's shirt again and threw him violently into the undergrowth. Then he dived in himself.

Just in time.

More bullets. These ones unquestionably close. Above the racket of discharging rounds, Norton let out a yell of pain and fright. King looked up and saw one of the bullets had grazed his shoulder, tearing out a small chunk of skin. Blood flowed from the hole in his shirt. It would hurt like hell, most definitely. But it wasn't the worst injury he could have sustained.

King waited for a lapse in the gunfire. When it came, he seized Norton and powered forward, putting distance between them and the clearing. He ignored Norton's cries of protest.

'This is for your own good,' he muttered as he spurred the boy ahead.

Before too long there came the familiar noise of the Super Stallion from somewhere near the trees ahead. The deep thrumming that King could feel in his chest. Once again, he noted it came from the same level that they were on, meaning it had descended for the second time.

He hoped for Norton's sanity that it stayed put.

As soon as the situation became apparent, King swore under his breath. He saw where the Super Stallion was, and realised he wasn't sure if Norton could go through with what they would have to do next.

Up ahead, the rainforest floor abruptly ceased. King realised that the whole time they had been heading for the edge of an enormous, sloping valley. This particular section of the rim was nothing but jagged cliff-face. There was a drop — large enough to be fatal — to the valley floor far below. The Super Stallion hovered in thin air, only a few feet away from the cliff's edge. There was no room to land on the cliff itself. The tree line ran right up to where the rock fell off into nothingness. The chopper's fuselage door lay wide open. Welcoming them.

'Oh, fuck,' Norton said as the realisation dawned. 'King, I can't jump. I can't fucking do that. I'd rather be shot again.'

'Trust me … no you wouldn't.'

'I—'

'Shut up, Ben. You're jumping. It's not even that far. Ready?'

'No.'

'Too bad.'

King made sure his grip was tight on Norton's shirt. If he let go, the boy might not commit to the action. Then he would be shot by the pursuing Phantoms, or worse ... taken alive.

He broke into a sprint for the edge of the cliff. Norton screamed as he was dragged along. King felt his knuckles go white. He embraced the stomach drop that came with such a brash decision. Fear of heights was a strange phenomenon. Getting shot at was a hundred times more dangerous than what he was about to do, yet this made him sweat. This made his skin crawl.

He reached the tipping point. Now there was no time to stop, even if he wanted to. If he slowed down he would skid off the edge of the cliff. He took another few steps, then thrust Norton out in front. The boy leapt with everything he had, clearing the distance between the cliff and the chopper easily. He crashed down on the floor of the fuselage.

King followed in his path, taking a deep breath and launching off the edge. A stray bullet from the trees behind made him flinch as he jumped. Instinctively, he looked down. His gut sank. The trees were nothing but dots far below. For a fleeting moment he arced through the air, the wind battering against him. Then he joined Norton inside the chopper, landing hard on his knees and skidding to a halt. Safe and sound.

It was only then that he realised the interior was empty. The four Delta Force soldiers were nowhere to be seen. He should have put two and two together earlier, but adrenalin had caused his attention to waiver. He hadn't even taken a glance inside the Super Stallion before he jumped.

He rolled over. Perhaps the pilot could explain.

As the cockpit came into view, he knew the pilot never would.

The pilot was dead.

His corpse lay beside King, a fresh bullet wound resting between his eyes. The small circular hole dripped a steady stream of blood, already pooling around his head. King looked past him, into the cockpit. He saw a man in the pilot's seat, and instantly recognised him. There was no mistaking the chiseled brown arms, the dreadlocks, the permanent sneer.

Mabaya.

CHAPTER 32

King made to scramble to his feet, but Mabaya stopped him in his tracks with a single gesture. The man leant over and brought his left arm into view, previously hidden behind the cockpit wall. King saw a small round object clasped between his fingers.

'Holy shit,' he muttered.

Mabaya was holding a live grenade. He couldn't make out the exact type, but there was no mistaking what it was. The safety pin had been withdrawn and Mabaya's fingers were pressed hard against the lever. If he released them even slightly, the grenade would detonate. The Super Stallion would be nothing but a flaming wreckage within seconds.

Norton saw the grenade too. He visibly paled, but didn't make a sound. Perhaps too shocked to speak.

'Didn't see that one coming, did you?' Mabaya said, cackling. 'Ah, you were so close, buddy. So close. You too, you little prick.' He nodded at Norton.

'You'd kill yourself just to stop us?' King said. 'We just wanted to leave.'

Mabaya turned to face him. There was pure, blind hatred in his eyes.

'You just wanted to leave?' he snarled. 'If you just wanted to leave, you would have left already. But you didn't. You had to come back and destroy fucking everything we'd been working for. So yes, I would kill myself right now to stop you. I'm gonna go land back at base and rip your fucking limbs off one at a time.'

'Maybe I'll just charge you now. Save the torture.'

'But you won't, American. I know you too well. You're the hero type. You always think there's a way out of everything. So you'll do whatever the fuck I say as long as I'm holding this thing.'

King sank to the floor. 'How did you even—'

'Ah, you thought I was just some dumb druggie, huh? I've served my time, same as you. Even flew a few helis in the Peruvian military. You caught me by surprise in the holding cell, but that doesn't make me a rookie. I lay in wait for the chopper, back in the clearing. I knew where they'd land. They opened the doors without a care in the world. I put a whole magazine into the four of them. The pilot wasn't armed. Finished him off with my sidearm. None of them ever saw it coming.'

King pressed his fingers into his eyes. Maybe if he'd just left the compound alone, none of this would have happened…

'What's wrong?' Mabaya said. 'Thinking about your friends? I saw their badges, by the way. Delta Force. I thought those guys were all smart and shit. A drug dealer outsmarted all of you! You must feel pretty fucking stupid right about now.'

Mabaya worked the controls and the Super Stallion began to move. He flew it low over the treetops, heading for the compound.

'Back to base,' he muttered, barely audible. 'Back to base we go. You two are so dead.'

'Mabaya,' King said, interrupting the man's ramblings.

He looked back. 'What, you pig?'

'You said you used to be a soldier. I'm a soldier. Man to man, we can work this out. Leave the kid out of it.'

Mabaya wagged a finger on his free hand. 'I left the army to get away from men like you, chicken shit. Men who think they're so fucking superior. So noble. *Leave the boy out of it. Waagh!'* He mocked King in a high-pitched tone, feinting distress. 'You will both die. Slowly. Nothing's fair out here. We're in the jungle, baby. Money's all that matters, and you fucked up what we were rolling in. Now you'll pay.'

King looked out the open fuselage door. In the distance, a plume of black smoke spiralled into the clouds. The warehouse, still ablaze. Quickly, he calculated their position based on the compound's location. If he was right, they should be over the...

He got to his feet.

Instantly Mabaya spun in his seat. 'Get the fuck back on the floor or I'll let go.' He waved the grenade for added effect.

'But you won't,' King said.

'Huh?'

'King, please get down,' Norton said from the back of the fuselage.

'No, Norton,' he said. 'Get up instead.'

'I'm not kidding!' Mabaya screamed. 'I'll let go!'

'No. You won't.'

Silence. King let a wry smile creep across his face. He'd successfully called the bluff.

'Like you said, this is all about money. You're not willing to kill yourself over it. I know that. You know that.'

Mabaya still said nothing.

'We're going to jump out now,' King said. 'And there's really nothing you can do to stop us.'

'We're doing what?' Norton said, flabbergasted.

'If you move a muscle, I let go,' Mabaya said in a desperate attempt to remain in control of the situation.

'I don't think you will. Ben, jump.'

'Wha—?'

'We're above the river. Jump now.'

Norton realised the urgency of what King had said. They wouldn't be in this position for long. They had a narrow window of opportunity. He had to take it.

King watched him suck in air, working up the nerve to act. Then he leapt out the open door and disappeared from sight.

Mabaya kept his hand wrapped firmly around the grenade. Now, King knew for sure he would not let go. Hesitation had backed him into a corner. He'd psyched himself out. He wouldn't be releasing that lever anytime soon. He let go of the controls and the Super Stallion drifted to a standstill in the air.

'This has backfired on you, hasn't it?' King said, still smiling.

'You jump into that river...' Mabaya said, his hand shaking. 'And I'll just land this thing and hunt you down and beat you to death.'

'I don't think you'll get the chance.'

King crossed to the open door, feeling the wind against his face. He glanced down at the flowing river beneath. There was Ben, bobbing on the surface. Alive. He stepped back inside the fuselage and wrenched something off the wall.

'You'll regret it if you jump,' Mabaya snarled.

'Doubt it.'

King unscrewed the plastic cap on the emergency flare he'd removed from the wall. He spun the cap between his fingers and struck the tip with the other end. Red sparks showered the fuselage and the flare hissed loudly, audible even over the din of the rotors. He stepped out into the open air, at the same time tossing the flare underhand into the cockpit.

CHAPTER 33

His stomach dropped as he fell. The Super Stallion shrank from sight until it was far overhead. King turned in the air and just had time to enter a pin drop position before he sliced into the murky water. The cold hit him hard. For a moment, he saw nothing but black. Then he kicked twice and surfaced.

Norton was treading water a few dozen feet away. King made eye contact with him, then looked up at the gargantuan vehicle hovering above their heads. It rested in place, not moving. A cloud of bright red smoke seeped from the open fuselage.

The whole world stood still.

'What did you do?' Norton said.

'Swim,' King said. 'Swim right now.'

Too late.

There came a deafening *bang* from overhead as all the windows of the cockpit were blown out. Grenades didn't create a fireball, contrary to popular belief. They simply caused massive instantaneous damage to anything in the general vicinity. King saw the Super Stallion quiver under the force of the detonation. Mabaya had done what King thought he would. He'd panicked, choking on flare fumes. And in the confusion he'd let go of the one thing keeping him alive.

The internal systems would be fried, demolished beyond repair. King stayed deathly still in the water. He hadn't anticipated what would probably come next. If he was lucky, everything would be okay.

He wasn't lucky.

The rotors slowed down, killed by the destruction of the onboard electronics.

With a groan, the Super Stallion tilted forward and fell like a boulder.

'*Down!*' King roared, his brain flooding with terror. Nothing sparked the nerves quite like an out of control fifteen-tonne steel wrecking ball.

There wasn't enough time to clear the impact zone by moving laterally. The Super Stallion was too large, too wide. King knew their only hope of survival was putting enough water above them to slow the destroyed chopper.

Norton had reacted faster than he thought he would. The boy was already underwater. King took one last look at the Super Stallion's nose, growing closer fast, and dove under the surface.

After the thunderous noise of the grenade blast, the silence under the river felt eerie. King twisted his body so that his head faced the river floor and kicked hard. Powerful, desperate strokes. Aiming straight down. He had roughly two or three seconds before the Super Stallion hit the water. In the muffled quiet, he heard his heart pounding in his chest, throbbing in his ears.

Was this the end?

He couldn't see, couldn't hear. He had no idea where Norton was. He could only descend. Another double-footed kick, another couple of metres toward the muddy bottom of the river.

Lungs aching.

Shoulder burning.

Head throbbing.

There was an enormous impact above, like a bass drum tearing through King's chest. Fifteen tons of metal hitting the surface. He heard it, but saw nothing. With no knowledge of whether he had done enough to get clear, he kicked a final time and braced himself for whatever happened next.

The wreckage smashed into him with indescribable force.

For a brief moment, he thought he'd made it far enough away from the impact zone. He hadn't. The water above him definitely slowed the chopper's descent; otherwise, he would have been killed upon impact. The Super Stallion broke through the water just slow enough so that King felt every ounce of it crushing his back, tearing every last bubble of air from his lungs, throwing him off to the side, spinning helplessly.

It felt like he'd been hit head on by a freight train.

He came to a halt underwater moments later, every single nerve ending screaming in pain. He knew he was still conscious, and he thought he might be paralysed. He prayed he wasn't. If his legs didn't work he would try helplessly to reach the surface, lungs slowly failing, vision slowly dimming, until his air finally ran out and he succumbed to drowning.

He kicked, ignoring the voice in his head that told him to just give up, to stop fighting against the pain, to let death take him so he could finally be relieved of the agony that had plagued him over the last twenty-four hours. His feet responded. He wasn't crippled. Not yet, anyway. Unaware of the extent of his injuries, he swam toward fresh air.

He broke the surface with a gasp. Beside him the Super Stallion rested vertically, its nose buried into the bottom of the river, its tail protruding from the surface. The tail rotor spun, still in the process of powering down. He saw Norton re-appear on the other side of the wreckage.

'Did it hit you?' King said, his voice quaking.

Norton shook his head. 'No.'

King sighed, relief flooding his thoughts. The boy was okay. That was all that mattered. 'Let's get to shore.'

They swam side-by-side, paddling for the riverbank. Norton looped a hand around King's waist, helping him along. He could tell King was seriously injured. When they crawled onto flat ground King collapsed into the mud, small waves still lapping at his torso. He rolled onto his back and stared up at the cloudless sky. By now the sun had fully risen and the jungle came alive with the sounds of wildlife. In any other scenario, it would be a pleasant setting.

'H-how bad are you hurt?' Norton stammered. He lay next to King, clutching his shoulder. It still ran with blood after being grazed by the bullet earlier.

'I don't know, kid,' King said, his eyes closed. 'Pretty bad.'

'Will you make it?'

'I hope so,' he said. He smiled, despite everything. 'Wouldn't be a great story if I finally finished what I set out to do and then dropped dead.'

Norton laughed. 'Is there more backup coming?'

'I hope so,' he said again.

'Do you still have that phone you used before?'

King reached down and patted his waistband, where he'd tucked the device in earlier that morning. He found nothing.

'It's gone. Must have slipped out somewhere. Let's hope whoever's coming knows where to look.'

He opened his eyes and looked at Norton. After everything that had happened, after all the death the boy had witnessed,

213

after all the injuries he'd sustained, he appeared to be doing okay. His expression was one of resignation. King knew he was in shock. When they were safe, the emotions would come flooding in.

For now, he would manage.

The pair lapsed into silence, watching the river flow past the demolished chopper. King dragged himself a little further up the riverbank. Pain receptors flared all over his body. He wasn't sure exactly where he was hurt the worst. It was impossible to pinpoint. Everything ached.

'Uh, King,' Norton said.

King looked at him. Norton was staring somewhere behind him, at the tree line. His face had turned paler than usual. Something was wrong. Hindered by his injures, King slowly craned his neck. Following Norton's gaze.

His heart skipped a beat.

Unarmed, unable to move, completely vulnerable, he watched as the two Phantoms who'd pursued them just minutes earlier stepped out of the jungle onto the riverbank. Both held their Kalashnikovs at shoulder height, barrels aimed directly at them.

There was no escaping this time.

CHAPTER 34

King took a deep breath. It could be the last he ever took. Beside him, Norton cried.

He saw the men pause. They observed the scene before them. The giant Super Stallion, demolished, buried in the river. The pair of helpless Americans resting on the shore. King saw something in their faces he didn't expect to see.

Hesitation.

One of them stepped forward. This man was tall and skinny, wearing a combat vest, khaki shorts and tattered trainers. He sported a buzzcut, hair shaved close to the skull. His eyes were wide with fear as he aimed his rifle at King.

'I speak English,' he said. 'Little bit.'

'What's your name?' King said.

'Paulo.'

'I'm Jason.'

'Where's Mabaya?'

King pointed at the Super Stallion. 'Somewhere in there. In a million pieces.'

'Dead?'

King nodded.

Paulo spent a moment mulling over what he had heard. Then he threw his gun away.

King found it hard to believe what he was seeing. The Phantom turned to his friend and barked a command in Spanish, and the second man also dropped his weapon. Paulo remained where he stood, contemplating what to do next.

'Do you have weapon on you?' he said in broken English.

King did his best to raise his hands. It hurt like hell, but he had to prove he was telling the truth. 'No weapons. I'm done.'

'I'm done too.'

Paulo began to descend the riverbank. His trainers flooded with mud, but he didn't seem to care. He stumbled alongside King and dropped to the ground. He stared out across the river.

'Why did you do that?' King said.

'What is point?' Paulo said. 'I kill you, your friends come and kill me. They know where we are. Why more death?'

King was taken aback by the sentiment, but he didn't let it show. 'Do you understand why I did what I did?'

'Of course,' Paul said, nodding. 'We take your friends. We kill some of them. No excuse.'

King stayed quiet.

'Do you know why we do that?' Paulo said.

King shook his head. 'No, I don't.'

'We die otherwise. No other jobs. Mabaya tell us what to do. If we don't, he kill us.'

'All of you?' King said.

Paulo shook his head. 'Most of them want to do this. This man, Marco—,' Paulo said, pointing to the second Phantom, '— he is my brother. We did not. We thought we would die. But we have to do what Mabaya say. Only way we get paid.'

'There's other ways to make money.'

'Not for us,' Paulo said. 'He kill my family.'

Paulo bowed his head and began to sob. King laid a hand on his shoulder. 'It's okay. I'll make sure you two are safe.'

'How?'

'I know people.'

Paulo turned to Norton. 'I am sorry.'

Norton didn't respond. King could tell the boy did not know what to say. But there was something resembling understanding in his eyes. Norton could see the pain on Paulo's face.

'What happens now?' Paulo said.

King made to respond, but felt the blood drain from his head. A wave of exhaustion fell over him. The trees and the mud and the water blurred into a kaleidoscope of bright colours and he felt his head drop back against the shore. He gratefully passed out.

CHAPTER 35

He came to surrounded by the roar of a helicopter.

The world felt distant. Still feeling the effects of his unconscious spell, King watched a UH-60 Black Hawk touch down on the mud a dozen feet away from them. Norton, Paulo and Marco sat still as the rotors powered down and the fuselage door slid open. Three Delta Force soldiers stepped down and headed for their position, all dressed in combat attire and clutching identical Colt M4 carbine rifles.

Paulo began to shake uncontrollably.

'Don't worry,' King said. 'Trust me, you'll be fine.'

When the group reached them, one soldier stepped forward. 'Jason King?'

King nodded.

The soldier extended a hand. King took it and was pulled to his feet. He winced in pain.

'My name's Barnes,' the man said. 'We've been sent in to assist with the extraction and lock down the area.'

'There's nothing left to lock down.'

Barnes hesitated. He looked out across the river and noticed the end of the Super Stallion rocking gently in the current. 'Is that—?'

'The first five Delta soldiers who got here are all dead. Their bodies are somewhere near the compound. They were shot.'

'Hostiles?'

'All dead too.'

King noticed Paulo glance at him, surprised. He made sure not to react.

'Who are these two?' Barnes said, gesturing to Paulo and Marco.

'Civilians. I found them being kept hostage inside the warehouse. They won't talk. We'll give them a lift to Iquitos and let them go.'

'Shouldn't we take them to—?'

'And do what?' King interrupted. 'Interview them? They've been through enough. The Phantoms have been eradicated. There's nothing left to question them about.'

Barnes nodded. 'Very well. Where are the hostages?'

King pointed to Norton. 'Here's one. The other two didn't make it.'

Barnes bowed his head. After a moment, he looked up. 'Are you hurt?'

There was no need to be unnecessarily stoic. 'Yeah. I'll need a hospital when we get back to Iquitos.'

'Let's get you four back home.'

The three soldiers helped them into the Black Hawk. King was tentative as he climbed into the fuselage and dropped into one of the hard plastic seats. He fastened the safety belt across his waist and let his head fall back against the wall behind.

'What a day,' he muttered.

Norton collapsed in the seat beside him, exhausted too. Paulo and Marco sat opposite. Their expressions were fearful. King didn't blame them. For years they had probably been conditioned to treat any Americans as the enemy. Mabaya was unrelenting in his hatefulness, which King guessed rubbed off on his underlings. Now, here they were inside one of their enemy's helicopters, going off nothing but a promise from the man who had decimated their forces.

'I need to make a call,' King said as Barnes leapt into the fuselage.

The man nodded knowingly. He didn't know who King worked for, but he knew its authority trumped all other branches. He had been instructed to follow King's requests, no matter how ludicrous. A call was understandable. He unclipped a Garmin satellite phone from his belt — this one newer and cleaner than the battered old device King had used in the jungle — and handed it over.

King thumbed the same buttons and followed the same procedure as he had the previous evening, passing on his identification code and connecting to Lars.

The man answered before the first ring. 'Yes?'

'We lost the four Delta soldiers. And the pilot. They're all dead.'

'Fuck.'

'We've been extracted by a second crew. Did you send them?'

'As backup. Just to make sure things went smoothly.'

'Far from smooth, Lars. But all hostiles are eliminated. It'll be a mess down there.'

'We have cleaning crew.'

'Use them. That was messy. There's a lot of dead bodies.'

'It was brash to go on alone after the airfield attack. Delta are telling me you should have waited.'

'If I had, I can't say the boy would have made it out alive. I think they would have all been killed.'

'I agree. You're lucky we exist, King. Any other branch and you'd be held accountable. You'd probably spend the rest of your life in jail.'

'I know.'

'I'll make it all disappear. You did good, soldier. Patch yourself up and get back here as fast as you can.'

'Another mission?'

'Another mission.'

King ended the call and sighed. The world didn't wait for him to get better. Corrupt psychopaths kept doing their thing. As long as he was serving, the stream of assignments would not end. There was too much evil in the world.

He felt the familiar stomach drop as the chopper lifted off the ground and banked west, toward Iquitos. Paulo and Marco shared looks of astonishment as they gazed out across the sea of green treetops stretching as far as the eye could see. He imagined they didn't spend much time in helicopters. He saw a single tear roll down Paulo's cheek, and tried not to let one of his own out. This was a new life for the brothers sitting opposite him. A fresh start, free from the influence of the Phantoms. King hoped they would do something with it. He would not be around to see it.

As always, Black Force needed him.

CHAPTER 36

Secada Airport was quiet at ten in the morning. The Black Hawk touched down on the airfield an hour after it left the Amazon Rainforest. King looked out at the tarmac and in the distance saw the big blocky shape of the airport terminal. For much of the last twenty-four hours he had been sure he would never see civilisation again. He thought he would die out in the rainforest, alone and in pain.

Every now and then, he couldn't help but be grateful.

A white minivan sped towards the Black Hawk. It sported the airport's logo on its side. An official vehicle.

'Who's that?' King said to Barnes as they disembarked the chopper.

'I think the kid's parents arrived this morning. I'd say its them.'

The airport official driving the van stamped to a halt a dozen feet from them. The rear door of the van burst open and a middle-aged couple jumped out, both their faces distraught. They saw Norton and instantly the mother burst into tears. She was a small lady with a mousy complexion. There was unquestionable relief in her eyes. The father was a balding man who King could see struggling to maintain a stoic demeanour. It did not last. As soon as Norton saw his parents he took off across the tarmac and wrapped an arm around them both. They cried into his shoulders, pulling him tight. King watched the scene unfold with a certain disconnect.

He'd never had that kind of relationship.

Barnes laid a hand on King's shoulder. 'You think he's gonna be alright?'

King shrugged. 'I don't know. He saw a lot. But he's tough. He stuck with me the whole way.'

'He'd be dead if it wasn't for you.'

'Hopefully, he goes on to do great things,' King said. 'Then I can be that guy who saved Ben Norton.'

Barnes chuckled. 'Where are you off to now?'

'Hospital. Then the Pentagon.'

'More work?'

'As always.'

'I hope they're paying you well. Whoever they are...'

Norton's parents let go of their son and walked over to the two soldiers.

'How did you get him out?' the woman asked both of them. She didn't know who had saved her son. Just that he was safe. King knew he had to keep it that way.

'I hope you understand that we can't go into too much detail,' Barnes said. 'For operational security. But your boy is safe, ma'am. He's seen a lot, but he's safe. Take care of him.'

King turned to Barnes. 'You got this?'

Barnes nodded.

With that, King turned and climbed back into the Black Hawk.

'How much fuel have we got?' he asked the pilot.

'Enough to get you to the hospital.'

'Then let's go.'

The chopper's rotors powered up. There was nothing further left to say. He had done his job. Rescued Ben Norton. Now it was time to go. King never let himself get personally attached to anyone he saved. It was his job to extract them, nothing more.

Norton came running over to the chopper.

'You're out of here?' he said.

King looked down at him. 'I'm needed elsewhere.'

'I can't say thank you enough.'

'You don't need to.'

Norton held out a hand. King shook it. He held eye contact for a moment. 'Take care of yourself, Ben.'

'You too, King.'

They both could not put into words the bond they shared. Not many people experienced the fight for survival alongside each other. They would always remember that.

King nodded once more, then the Black Hawk lifted off the tarmac and moved laterally through the air.

Onto the next task.

Read Matt's other books on Amazon.

amazon.com/author/mattrogers23